Provocation

EXPLICITLY YOURS • BOOK THREE

JESSICA HAWKINS

Editing by Elizabeth London Editing
Proofreading by Tracy Seybold
Cover Design © OkayCreations.
Cover Photo © shutterstock.com/g/fotoduki

Provocation (EXPLICITLY YOURS SERIES 3)

ISBN: 0997869135
ISBN-13: 978-0-9978691-3-2

TITLES BY
JESSICA HAWKINS

LEARN MORE AT JESSICAHAWKINS.NET/BOOKS

SLIP OF THE TONGUE
THE FIRST TASTE
YOURS TO BARE

THE CITYSCAPE SERIES

COME UNDONE
COME ALIVE
COME TOGETHER

EXPLICITLY YOURS SERIES

POSSESSION
DOMINATION
PROVOCATION
OBSESSION

STRICTLY OFF LIMITS

Chapter One

Present day

Lola's heels clicked against the hallway's hardwood floors like the countdown of a ticking time bomb. Windows lined one side, and the rising sun striped the opposite wall with sharp-cornered shadows. The house, square between the curves of the Hollywood Hills, was renowned for its modern design. But Lola didn't see the appeal in a home that echoed her every move. To her, it was a shell—beautiful on the outside, hollow on the inside. Just like its owner.

She crossed the foyer on her way to the kitchen. At the entryway table, under the garish *Montgolfier* chandelier, she stopped to center a vase of Calla lilies—amongst such perfection, the slightest flaw glared. She slid a flower out of the arrangement and dragged her fingertip up its stem, bending it nearly to the point of snapping. Even the house's feminine touches were stiff.

Lola had once loved Calla lilies, especially the purple-hearted ones like this that were edged in white. But she'd learned to be wary of anything that thrived in such barren surroundings.

"You're up early," she heard from behind her.

Lola replaced the flower, slipping it back into its spot, and turned around. Beau leaned in the doorway, his suit straight and sharp, a newspaper folded under his arm.

She went to him. "I wanted to say good morning before you left."

He checked his watch. "By the skin of your teeth."

She smiled thinly. Beau was punctual. That was no surprise. But when she'd fantasized about spending a morning with him, it hadn't been anything like this—scrounging for extra minutes. Not that it really mattered.

She put slinky arms around his neck, drew his head down to hers. "Are you hungry? I can make you something quick."

"What do you think?" His voice deepened as he rested a hand on her lower back, at the base of her zipper. "I'm a man who hasn't eaten in almost three weeks."

Lola lingered a moment, their mouths close, prolonging a kiss that wasn't just a kiss. It was a sneak preview. A tease. A warning. She pressed her lips to his like a woman who didn't want her boyfriend to walk out the door. Like a woman in love.

When she pulled away, one corner of Beau's mouth curved into a smile. "Wow. Careful, or I won't be held responsible for breaking your rules."

She shrugged and fixed his tie, even though it was perfectly straight. "I've been thinking—about us." She glanced up at him from under her lashes. "About the rules."

He took a handful of her backside. "Probably not as much as I have."

"I'm ready, Beau. Tonight."

His expression didn't change, but she caught the slight twitch of his eye. "Don't tease me," he said. "It wouldn't be wise to put chocolate cake in front of a starving man."

Lola removed her arms to take his cheeks in her hands. "I know it's been difficult these past three weeks—"

"Two and a half."

This time, Lola flinched. As if she needed a reminder of how dangerous it could be to let her guard down for even a second. She ignored the comment. "You've been patient," she continued. "I haven't forgotten anything, but I'm ready to start moving forward."

With his hand on her ass, Beau pulled her against him, forcing her feet to shuffle forward the last few inches. "Why wait until tonight? I can be a couple minutes late."

Lola's heart hammered once, the way it always did when Beau got like this—impatient. He could be convincing in a way that was hard for her to resist, but she had to. Giving in to him now could unravel everything. "I want it to be special—not in the doorway on your way to work. You can survive until tonight."

"I'm not so sure about that," he said. "I've never slept next to the same woman this many nights in a row without so much as a handjob. It's miraculous I'm still upright."

Lola shook her head but smiled. "You are a true romantic, Mr. Olivier. I'm a lucky woman."

He put his knuckle under her chin to keep her eyes on him. "I'm the lucky one."

"Are you?" The words came out of her mouth too fast. Now, around him, she filtered everything. But today was a day she'd been anticipating for a while, and that alone was a reason to be even more careful.

Along with excitement came a tiny crack of doubt inside her, though. It was silly. She knew how Beau felt. He was happy she was there, even if he wasn't around all the time. He loved her, despite the fact that he hadn't told her. He didn't always show it, but she was his priority. She had to believe those things were true, because if not, then all this had been for nothing.

"Am I lucky?" he asked. "I've been given a second chance I didn't deserve. I thought I had it all, Lola, but I was coming home to an empty house. I just didn't realize that was a bad thing until I started coming home to you. I'm a lucky son of a bitch. And I'm the happiest I've ever been."

She glanced away, but only for a second—it was a telling habit she'd been trying to kick. Beau didn't consider himself romantic. Lola disagreed. The rest of the world could keep their flowers and candy. For her, Beau was taking a dull hammer to his brick walls, a slow process, but one that meant more to her than anything money could buy. It still wasn't enough.

Despite fighting herself every waking moment, she loved him. She couldn't have faked all the things she had without that. When he'd broken her heart, though, she'd buried that love—and she threw more dirt on it every day. Because Lola *wasn't* happy. And if Beau thought she was, then he didn't know her at all.

"I should get to the office," he said when she didn't respond. "The sooner this day is over, the sooner I'll be home with you."

Beau was sweeter in the morning, before the day had gotten to him. She didn't doubt he meant what he said, but during the week, he only came home at a decent time when they had an event to attend. Those nights, he was always standing too close, touching her somewhere, as if assuring himself she was real.

"Be home by seven o'clock." She didn't smile. She crossed her arms, tapping her index finger on her bicep. "And I don't mean *leave* work at seven. We have a reservation at seven-thirty."

"We do?"

"I told you last week I was making dinner plans and not to schedule anything."

"If I did, I'll cancel it. Now that I know what's in store for tonight." He tucked some of her hair behind her ear. She knew the low-lidded look he was giving her well—she got it several times a day. She'd asked him once what he was thinking about when he made that expression, and he'd just said, *"Us."*

5

"Listen—why don't you let my assistant handle tonight?" he asked. "Pick any restaurant, I don't care how exclusive. She'll make it happen. I want the best for…"

Lola stopped listening, pressing her lips together, her jaw tingling. She wanted to ask him what the hell made him think she'd prefer an expensive restaurant to anything else. Hell, an In-N-Out burger and a chocolate shake was enough to make her mouth water. Despite the staggering amount of cash she had stashed in a locker downtown, she was still the same Lola who wore beat-up Converse and regularly chose beer over wine.

"You surprised me with balcony seats to the ballet last week," Lola said, interrupting whatever he was saying. "I want to return the favor."

Beau arched an eyebrow. "It's a surprise?"

She smoothed her hand over his tie. "You're always in charge. Just relax. Let me do this for you."

"I like being in charge."

With the drop in his tone, an unexpected thrill ran up her spine. If Beau did one thing well, it was taking charge. That was how she'd ended up on her stomach on his hotel bed their second night together, letting him have her in ways Johnny hadn't in their nine years together. It was also the reason she had to be on alert at all times.

"At least let me send you a new dress," he said.

"If you keep buying me dresses, we'll have to add on another wing just to store them."

Beau smiled. "That can be arranged."

Lola had never owned so much in her life. But what was actually hers? Beau didn't like her to spend her own money. He thought she'd deposited it into a savings account where it was earning interest, and he'd made her promise she wouldn't use it. "Save it for something nice here and there," he'd said. As if 'something nice' was the *real* reason she'd accepted a million dollars to fuck him.

"I already have an outfit planned," Lola said slowly, "and I think you'll like it very much."

Beau ran his hand up over her backside, lingering, slow. There were some things she never had to fake, like swooning at his touch, or the gradual but electric creep of warmth it sent through her.

He liked the dress she'd chosen that morning. She could tell by the way he absentmindedly touched it while they talked—rubbing the soft wool, playing with the tail of the zipper. It was short, which was fine, because she had great legs, and the neckline was high. Conservative but sexy, the kind of woman Beau should have on his arm. Her leather pants were still stuffed at the bottom of her duffel bag, though to his credit, Beau had asked about them. He liked those too.

"What're your plans today?"

Lola lifted one shoulder. "Shopping. I have some small things to get for tonight."

"Good. Put everything on my card, all right? I don't want you spending money on me."

Had this been the special evening Beau thought it was, Lola would've given it more thought. She would've taken him up to Mulholland Drive, brought some hotdogs since they'd never gotten to eat theirs, played Pink Floyd on the car stereo and made love to him under the stars. Money wouldn't've even crossed her mind, but that was where Beau always went, and that was one of the reasons he and Lola were very, very different.

That was the life he'd chosen not to have with her. Lola agreed to charge her shopping to him—not because she felt good about spending his money, but because she'd cut up all except one of her credit cards the night before.

Beau leaned in, kissed her once on the lips and walked away. "Warner can take you today. I'll drive myself."

"Beau?"

He turned partway around and nodded at her. "Yeah?"

Lola's throat constricted, as if she physically couldn't speak. She had tried many times to tell him she loved him for the sake of making this work, but each time, she'd choked on the words. It was the truth, but it felt like a lie.

"Can I take the Range Rover?" she asked instead. She needed to be alone today, and while Beau's driver was good at blending into the background, he wasn't much for disappearing completely.

"Of course. You know you don't have to ask. But I don't mind driving—"

"I hate it." Lola sucked in a tiny breath. She was getting sloppy. She couldn't go around blurting things without thinking first.

Provocation

"You hate what?" He faced her completely, his attention snagged.

Being treated like a doll. Lavished with expensive things I don't care about. Sitting around all day, waiting for you to come home. "Warner driving me around," she said. "It feels extravagant."

He shrugged, his hands in his pockets. "Warner drives me all the time. It's more normal than you think."

"Maybe for people like you."

"People like me?" Beau tilted his head with interest. She would've preferred to drop it, though, this conversation they would've had if things had been different. If she cared about making this work. "You *are* people like me. Now."

Lola kept a poker face, even as her blood simmered a little. Letting her emotions get the best of her was the kind of thing that got her into trouble, but *that* pissed her off. She wasn't like him. She hadn't even wanted the money—she'd just been a pawn in a transaction between Johnny and Beau.

"I didn't mean it like that," Lola said, regaining her silky smoothness. "But it makes sense for you because you work in the car. I don't. I just sit and stare out the window, so I might as well drive myself."

"Fine," he said. "Take the Range Rover."

Lola walked over to him and touched his forearm. "Why don't you give Warner the day off? I'm sure he'd appreciate that."

"Why don't you just let me buy you a car?"

She smiled up at him. "Because there are two in the garage, and two people in this house. Again, extravagant."

"Better get used to it, *ma chatte*." He kissed her one more time. "I really have to run. See you tonight. Seven o'clock."

Beau walked out of the room, and she listened for the conclusion of the morning show—the rumbling garage door, the roar of the Lamborghini's engine. No matter where in the house she was—eating toast in the breakfast nook, staring at Beau's pillow in his bed—that was when everything in her body unclenched. Being around him was constant mental warfare.

Lola went into the kitchen to locate the keys to the Range Rover. This would be the one day she'd enjoy spending Beau's money. Her to-do list wasn't very long, but each thing was an important cog in her plan.

Not long ago, Beau's kitchen was the last place she thought she'd be standing. As she'd fled his hotel room, doing her best to hold her broken heart together, she'd never wanted to see Beau's face again—much less be living in his home. But this morning, knowing what was to come later that night, there was nowhere else she'd rather be. As it turned out, a hell of a lot could change in three weeks.

Chapter Two

Three weeks earlier

There was a reason Beau never thought about that night at Cat Shoppe. He'd pushed Lola—and the memory of her on stage—down into his depths years ago. She was never meant to surface. It should've been the best day of his life—selling his first company for millions after a decade of struggle. It would've been, had he just gone home after his last celebratory drink.

But he hadn't, and now he stood in the Presidential Suite at the Four Seasons, staring at the door Lola had just left through. Their words echoed through the hotel room—cold, hard confessions and accusations. His normally steady heartbeat raced as if he'd just run a sprint. It unnerved him. Remaining calm was something he'd trained himself to do, a survival tactic for situations like leading a boardroom full of megalomaniacs.

He couldn't—*wouldn't*—allow anyone that power

over him. She'd done him a favor by walking out before he could explain, opening his eyes when he'd been blind for her. What had he thought—that Lola was anything more to him than another challenge? The thing that'd made her special, that'd set her apart from other women, ceased to exist. She no longer had his power. It'd been a struggle, but he'd taken it back. Now, she was just another defeated opponent, a discarded chess pawn.

Beau returned to the suite's master bedroom. It was hot in the room, as if the heat had been on all night. As if it'd all been some sort of fever dream—intense, vivid, colorful. Over with the new day's dawn.

Except that Lola was everywhere in that hotel room. Her red lipstick, smeared into the comforter. His white robe that she'd worn, strewn across a chair. His tie, still knotted, on the floor where he'd discarded it after blindfolding her. She'd really gotten to him, burrowing deep, making him think the ending he'd planned wasn't what he wanted after all. It wasn't the first time she'd drawn him under her spell.

Ten years earlier, Beau had become the man he'd always wanted to be. Now, he and his money were respected in the business world. Sought after. The definition of power. And underneath it all had always been his weakness—the girl in the black kitten ears.

Beau crouched at the footboard and picked up the gold dress he'd ripped off her body. Beads bit into his palms when he squeezed it. No—none of it'd been a dream. Thrusting inside her, wondering how it was possible, with all the fucking he'd done in his life, that he'd never felt anyone that way—that was real.

It was real, the way she'd approached the gas station the night before, a small smile on her face, her eyes turned up slightly as if lost in a daydream. With a gun to his head, he couldn't move, couldn't scream at her to run, couldn't do anything but watch her pull open the door and step into a nightmare. He would've done anything to stop it, would've handed over everything he'd worked for, but he could only stand there.

Beau tossed the dress aside and stood, running his hands over his hair. He needed to get ready for his day. He and Lola were done—there was nothing more to say. Warner had her now, and she'd be home soon— getting her things, breaking Johnny's heart. Beau hoped she'd be brutal. No man should get off easy for selling the woman he claimed to love.

He thought about calling Warner and telling him to stay with Lola. When she was finished, she'd need to leave quickly, shed that sorry excuse for a boyfriend. Warner could drop her off—where? It occurred to him she might not have anywhere to go. That she'd get in Warner's car and feel like she had no one. That she might not get in Warner's car at all. That without a reason to leave, she might—stay. With Johnny.

Across the room, Beau's cell was in pieces on the floor from when he'd hurled it at the wall. He went for the hotel phone. He was unreachable, having instructed the front desk to hold his calls so his time with Lola wouldn't be interrupted.

He began to dial Warner. Just because he didn't want Lola didn't mean he wanted her staying with

Johnny. This part was easy for Beau, anyway. With one phone call and a little cash, Warner would handle it. Whatever Lola needed—a ride, a hotel room for a few days, a new job—Beau could give it to her without even a word between them.

He paused, his finger hovering over the last number. His heart beat hard enough for him to notice. Lola wasn't his problem to fix. And like Beau had told her—he wasn't Johnny. He didn't waver in his decisions. He didn't backtrack. The game was over, and Warner was returning Lola to the past where she belonged. There'd be other women to fuck after an expensive dinner, new challenges to hold his interest, more ways to buy what he wanted. She had the money if she got into trouble. She didn't need Beau. And he—he had an empire to run.

Beau set the receiver back on its cradle and glanced out the door of the balcony. The sun was cresting over the mountains. From the start, Beau had always known there'd be a moment when it would all come to an end. This was that moment.

Chapter Three

It'd all started with a look.

Lola had stepped out from behind Cat Shoppe's curtains, center stage, the night's main feature. Nineteen, lithe and limber, but what'd set her apart most was that she'd loved to dance—the owner's words. Then again, the other girls had been at it much longer, and they'd seen a lot more than her. If they'd ever loved to dance, maybe they'd found more reasons not to.

Seconds into her number, she'd glanced over her shoulder and met eyes with a strikingly handsome man who looked sorely out of place and with no clue about it. That man would change the course of her life. He'd buy her body for a night, and then he'd buy her heart, and that would bring her to this moment—arms full of money, legs stretching wider with each step. Unable to get away fast enough.

The doorman just barely pulled the handle in time to let her out. She fled the Four Seasons hotel. The

Beverly Hills concrete was smooth under her Converse, the opposite of the sidewalks around her apartment.

"Wait!" a male voice cried behind her. She stopped. The sun was still behind the mountain, but it would be up soon. She turned around, squinting at the figure jogging toward her in the semi-dark, waving his arms.

Lola would've reveled in the pitiful display if the man was Beau, but he wasn't. Beau would never run after anything—or anyone. Not that it mattered. If Beau wanted something badly enough, he'd catch it anyway.

She recognized Beau's driver as he slowed to a stop in front of her, his breathing labored. "I'm supposed to take you home, Miss Winters." He straightened his tie and left it even more crooked. With a nod back toward the hotel, he said, "I have the car waiting. I'm to take you home and stay out front until you're ready to come back here."

Lola's broken heart ached a quick second, a longing sigh. That'd been their plan, made only minutes ago, and it'd seemed solid. She and Beau were upside down, inside out, backward—and, somehow, they were just right. Until the truth had dropped into the room, diffusing their fantasy future like it'd been nothing more than a cloud.

Lola narrowed her eyes at Warner. Her disgust for Beau branched out, disfigured fingers on a dying tree, looking to take anything down with it. "Is that what you're *to do*?"

He looked from side to side without moving his head a millimeter. "Um—Mr. Olivier called about fifteen minutes ago and specifically instructed—"

"Mr. Olivier can instruct his foot up his ass. Take another step toward me, and I'll scream."

Warner swayed back as if she'd swung at him. "Excuse me?"

"I'll find my own way." Lola turned back around. She and Beau no longer owed each other anything, not even a lift home. She started the two-something mile walk back to her apartment.

Innumerable customers had passed through during the two years she'd stripped at Cat Shoppe. It was a wonder she remembered that particular night at all, but she did. That man across the club had worn a suit, not unusual for their clientele. Cat Shoppe had been more exclusive in those days. He'd been older to her then, but now she just recalled him as smooth and spotless. Not the hard, angular man he was now. How she could've forgotten Beau's bottomless green eyes, she wasn't sure, but she'd tried not to look too hard into anyone's eyes when she'd worked there.

He'd stayed near the entrance, watching her. She'd been stared at before, but this was different. It was the same feeling she'd gotten on the sidewalk at Hey Joe— as if he'd been passing by and something had stopped him in his tracks.

Backstage, the owner, Kincaid, had pulled her aside and sent her to the VIP room. At first, Beau hadn't demanded anything or tried to grope her. He'd seemed more interested in talking. He'd looked into her eyes when speaking to her, not at her tits. Although, he'd looked at those too. Beau was right that she'd brushed against him when she'd danced for him, even though that wasn't allowed.

And then, out of nowhere, he'd offered her money to go home with him—and doused any interest she'd had. It was presumptuous, and in a way, disappointing. Up until then, she'd been a girl intrigued, wanting to know more about this man who wasn't like the others who paid for time alone with her. As if it'd been some warped version of a first date.

He'd left abruptly after she'd turned him down, and she'd forgotten it by the next day.

Beau hadn't. Her rejection had struck something deep inside him—something that'd compelled him to lead her right into the mouth of a fire just to watch her burn. It didn't matter that he'd changed his mind at the end. It only took one ember to send everything up in flames.

She'd had this sick fullness in her gut before—an unruly customer pulling down her thong during a lap dance. She'd knocked the scrawny guy on his ass with a lucky punch. When one of her mom's boyfriends had struck her, she'd launched toward him, claws out. She would've lost if her mom hadn't stepped in, but that didn't matter. Both times, she'd fought back.

Lola readjusted the package of cash in her arms. The sun's fiery-orange arch peeked on the horizon, silhouetting palm trees. Even though she had the money—the money was *all* she had—she refused to get a cab. In her eyes, it was no different than accepting a ride from Beau.

Besides, the sooner she got home, the sooner she'd have to face Johnny. It wouldn't be difficult to hide what she'd done—declaring her love for the enemy. She doubted Johnny'd even think to ask. The problem was that she'd meant it. No matter how badly Beau had hurt her, love didn't come with an off switch. She couldn't go home to Johnny and pretend none of it'd ever happened. And after what she'd been through with Beau, she wasn't sure she wanted to anyway.

She and Beau were fire and ice. They were never meant to be together. They clashed. They exploded. He heated her when she was cold and soothed her when she was burning up. That couldn't be faked. In the convenience store, with a gun under her chin, Beau wouldn't let the man take her outside where Beau couldn't see her.

Johnny wasn't a protector. The moment Beau's business card had gone missing from Hey Joe's countertop, her trust in Johnny had begun to chip away—a gradual process she hadn't even been completely aware of.

The first night, as she'd approached the limo idling at the curb of her apartment complex, Beau'd rolled down the window and looked up at her. Johnny had watched from the window. She'd had no idea the two men would each tear out half her heart, leaving a gaping wound in its place. She'd had no idea that as much as Johnny had loved her, and as much as Beau would worship her, it would end this way.

Lola picked up her pace, flexed her weighed-down muscles. Half a million dollars was fucking heavy.

Hadn't she been good to both of them? For Beau, she'd risked everything. For Johnny, she'd given him whatever he'd wanted the last nine years. She hadn't asked for much in return. Just to be safe, loved—to be enough.

She wasn't safe. She wasn't enough. And now, she didn't have anyone. Beau had taken all that away from her. But as sure as that money in her arms, she was still standing. They'd landed their punches, but neither of them had knocked her off her feet.

It wasn't over yet, though. Lola and Johnny still had to face the truth. They'd made a deal with the devil, and the devil was cashing in. From Lola, he would take her heart. From Johnny, he would take Lola.

Chapter Four

Beau strained his hands against the fabric of his trouser pockets as the elevator leveled with the hotel's ground floor. He hadn't slept a wink, but when the doors opened, he straightened his shoulders and strode out like he would any other day. Because it was any other day. There was nothing particularly special about this one, except for his early-morning meeting with Mayor Churchill—a meeting he'd been trying to get for some time, and one he wouldn't have without Lola's help. At least she'd been good for that.

"Good morning, Mr. Olivier."

He smiled at the familiar face behind the front desk. "Morning, Heather."

"New tie?"

Beau touched the knot at the base of his neck. "Thank you for noticing."

"I always do. How'd you sleep?"

As he passed, Beau rapped his knuckles against the counter and winked. "Like a baby. Cab's out front?"

"Yes, sir."

Living in a hotel had its perks. Being greeted in the mornings by the Four Seasons' model-actress concierge, Heather, should've been one of the best. But the quickest way to turn Beau off was to make it easy for him. Girls like Heather had become a dime a dozen the day he'd put on a bespoke Prada suit and stepped onto the sidewalk of Rodeo Drive.

The attention had been fun at first, but the appeal had worn off quickly. It'd been some time since Beau'd picked up a random girl for a night, but he figured after what he'd been through the last twenty-four hours, maybe it was just what he needed. A nap, a strong drink and a good, meaningless fuck. Not necessarily in that order.

Out front, Warner waited at the passenger's side of his town car, his expression typically stoic. Beau'd worked with the man ten years, though, and he sensed something was off when Warner didn't jump to get the car door for Beau.

"I already arranged a ride," Beau said, checking his watch—6:56 A.M. Approximately thirty minutes since Lola had bolted from his room. "I thought you'd be longer."

"I tried calling. Miss Winters refused a ride home."

Beau slowed to a stop. "Did she?"

"Yes, sir."

Beau blew out a heavy sigh. Of course she had. Lola could be stubborn and proud—a potentially self-destructive mix. "I take it you put her in a cab?"

"She walked."

Beau's body locked up. The hotel's sidewalk curved along the driveway and disappeared behind a wall of greenery. When she'd left, the sky had still been dim. Beverly Hills or not, she shouldn't have been walking alone at that hour. Especially not with all that cash. He didn't like it.

"What the hell were you thinking letting her walk?" Beau asked.

"Sir, with all due respect, I've never given any of your dates a ride home. I didn't think you'd mind." Warner's mouth twitched at the corner. "And she can be very convincing."

Beau raised his chin. It was true. When Beau spent the night with a woman, he'd usually send her off with more than enough cash for a cab and didn't think of it again. He flexed his fingers, which he didn't remember curling into fists. "Of course. You're right. She'll be fine."

Warner moved to get the car door for Beau. "We could probably still catch her."

Beau unbuttoned his blazer. Lola was a smart girl. She wouldn't put herself in danger. And if she did, that was Johnny's problem, not Beau's. He got into the backseat. "I can't be late for this meeting. Miss Winters will have to handle herself from here on out."

"Very well, sir." Before Warner closed the door, he cleared his throat. "If you'd like, I can drop you off and go look myself. I didn't mean to imply she's just another—"

"I said no." Beau sniffed. "Don't bring it up again."

Warner nodded and shut the door.

Beau'd had enough of thinking and talking about Lola. She'd made the choice to walk out when he'd asked her to stay and trust him. Maybe that was a lot to expect, but he'd deserved that little bit of faith after what they'd been through. Beau looked out the window and tried to focus on his upcoming meeting. He wanted to be done with Lola, wanted her out from under his skin. All the more reason to find himself a Heather for a night—and soon.

What Beau didn't expect to find was someone better than the attention-hungry Heathers he normally met. Upon entering Mayor Churchill's City Hall office, he was *not* greeted by a pretty, young brunette. She didn't even look up from her computer when he approached her desk.

"Appointment?" she asked, clicking her mouse furiously.

"Yes, I have an appointment," Beau said deliberately. "Beau Olivier."

She glanced up for a brief moment and then away. "I'll let the mayor know. You can take a seat."

She had long, dark hair and fair skin. There was skepticism in her blue eyes—of him, of everything around her. She resembled Lola enough that he didn't want to stop talking to her.

"Mind if I stand?" he asked. "I'm not very good at sitting still."

"Makes no difference to me."

"I could use a coffee," Beau said. "Didn't have time to stop."

She sighed, finished whatever she was typing and left the room.

She was clearly annoyed with him, and Beau loved every moment. He glanced at her computer clock. He had four minutes before the meeting began. It could be done. He'd turned a girl from cold to hot in less time.

She returned and handed him a paper cup. "I hope you like it black. We're out of creamer."

"It's perfect—" He stooped to read the nameplate on her desk and chuckled. "Heather. Is that your real name?"

"What kind of a question is that?" she shot back.

"Never mind. Have you worked here long?"

"Yes." She scratched her neck, leaving a bright red mark on her skin. Just like Lola, her throat was long, slender and pale.

"You must really love your work," Beau said. "You've barely taken a second to breathe."

"I do."

When she didn't continue, Beau asked, "Why? What do you love about it?"

She blinked a few times at the screen and stopped typing. "Well, Mayor Churchill's so—I really like working for him."

"How come?" He craned his neck to the side to catch her eye. "A lot of people actually hate working for politicians."

"That's just it," she said quickly, turning to him finally, her expression brightening. "He's not your typical politician. The mayor's very dedicated to this city. It's an honor to be on his team. When I was young, I wanted to be an elementary school teacher, but then I took this poly-sci class in school, and it's so weird, because…"

Beau was sure it was weird, but he didn't care. He stopped listening. It turned out that almost-black hair, blue eyes and a white throat didn't mean anything. But that was the point, wasn't it?

He smiled at her, nodded.

Heather was still talking when he looked up to find Churchill standing in the doorway of his office, watching them. He straightened up. "Good morning, Mayor."

"Glenn is fine." He stepped aside. "Come on in, Olivier. About time we did this."

"I agree." Beau crossed through reception and shook his hand.

"Thank you, Heather," the mayor said, inviting Beau into his office with an open arm. He shut the door behind them and rounded his desk to sit behind it.

"Mayor—Glenn, thanks again for clearing time in your schedule to see me," Beau started. "This meeting isn't about you or me. It's about Los Angeles. Together, we can—"

Churchill held up a hand. "Slow down, Olivier. It's not even eight in the morning yet." He picked up a mug with a large, black mustache printed on the side. Before taking a drink, he held it out and nodded. "Isn't that something? Got it for Christmas last year from my nieces. Makes me look like I've got facial hair when I drink out of it. Watch."

Beau shifted in his chair as Churchill took a sip, the mustache lining up right under his nose.

Churchill swallowed, raised the mug and laughed as he reclined back against his seat. "Isn't that something," he repeated. "Got any plans for the weekend?"

"No, sir. Just work."

"Work? You're not serious."

"The way I see it, Saturday's just another day to get things done," Beau said. "Every day might as well be Monday to me."

"Huh." Churchill nodded slowly, studying his coffee a moment. He raised his eyebrows at Beau. "That's a shame. Saturday mornings, Lois and I like to take a walk through the neighborhood, get some fresh air while it's quiet out. Then we meet friends at a Santa Monica-based coffee shop and roaster. If we aren't careful, we'll sit there all day talking about absolutely nothing."

Beau smiled. It was a nice picture, but it wasn't him. And it had nothing to do with why he was there. "I'm glad to hear you support small businesses in the area. I try to do the same. Just like the talent coming out of our universities that I'd like to keep here in Los Angeles." He sipped his coffee.

"How's Lola?"

Beau coughed, nearly spitting out his drink. *Lola?* Gone, that's what she was. Out of his life for good. And she needed to stay gone. Beau'd watched Churchill fall in love with Lola the night of the gala—her spunk, her fire had worked on him. He didn't blame the poor man. If she could sucker Beau into falling for her, then Churchill had no chance.

Beau opened his mouth to answer and quickly decided to use this to his benefit. He cleared his throat. "She's doing well. Keeping busy."

"I imagine she'd have to if you're working weekends."

Beau pursed his lips at the thought of having an entire weekend with Lola. Even though he'd spent nearly every morning the last few years working, it wasn't that difficult to picture it—driving to Venice Beach with the top down, enjoying the sun and breeze, eating ice cream cones on the boardwalk. Things he hadn't done in years and years. He ran his hand along the arm of his chair. "I make time for her too."

"I don't know what it is," Churchill said. "There's just something about her that's stuck with me. Think it's that she reminds me a little of my wife when we were younger. I asked Lois out probably ten times before she finally gave in just to shut me up."

"I'm sure she's thankful you were so persistent."

"My wife is the most amazing woman I know," he continued. "You probably think I'm an old fool to say this, but I believe it—the caliber of woman a man chooses to have by his side says a great deal about how he does business."

Beau looked down into his coffee. That was one of the many differences between Lola and the Heathers of the world. Lola wasn't insecure, but she was even more than what she gave herself credit for. Beau'd seen that even from across the room when he'd entered that strip club. No matter how much he tried to forget her or how angry he was, he couldn't take that from her. She would always be that caliber of woman.

Beau shook his head a little. "I don't think I need to tell you that it's rarely a man who chooses a woman. It's the other way around."

The mayor laughed. "How right you are. Especially a woman like that. I said it once, but I'll say it again— don't let go of that one."

A memory hit him hard, flooding into the tiny cracks in his resolve. Lola in his arms as they'd stood on his hotel room balcony the night before. He'd held her tightly, afraid he wouldn't be ready to let her go when the sun rose. He shut the thought down, refocusing on Churchill. "You're a busy man, Mayor. I am too. Should we get started?"

"I've been paying attention to you since our dinner," Glenn said. "You have an impressive track record, Olivier. When you choose a company, it almost always succeeds. What's your secret?"

Finally, a topic Beau was happy to distract himself with. "It's the other way around, actually. I choose them because they're poised for success. It's all about meticulous research. At the firm, I make sure we cover all our bases. We pore over numbers, we do case studies, we submerge ourselves in the markets."

"Sure, sure," Churchill said, waving a hand. "But it's more than that for you, isn't it?"

Beau set his coffee on the desk. "I'm sorry. I don't think I understand the question."

"You have an unorthodox way of dealing with the founders of the companies you invest in. Instead of sending your employees in your place or just gathering research online, you spend weeks courting them, getting to know them firsthand."

"That's all true."

"You're not investing in these companies. You're investing in the people."

"Well, businesses don't run without people. I vet them thoroughly, which is why I'm so confident in my portfolio." Beau slid the end of his tie through his hand. "As a result, the returns have been staggering."

"Beau," Glenn said, dropping his smile. "Be straight with me. I looked into your background. It took some digging, but I found that yearly conference thing you do. You never mentioned it before."

"It's no secret that Bolt Ventures sponsors *Entrepreneurs in Tech*."

"Not just sponsors. You and your company put it on, every last detail."

Beau nodded slightly. In fact, he'd even helped design the conference's lunch menu, since he'd been the one paying for it. "It's important. To us. And me."

"What I don't understand is why your name wasn't front and center on the project. What do you get out of it if not publicity? What's your concern with young, struggling entrepreneurs like the ones behind these companies you endow?"

Beau released his tie. He had answers prepared for everything. He liked having the right response, one he'd perfected over the years based on people's reactions. He never lied, but how you said things was sometimes more important than what you said. People picked up on keywords, tone, delivery.

Churchill wasn't responding to that. He valued truth and authenticity. Those were things Glenn'd seen in Lola, and they were the reasons she'd 'stuck with him.' Beau knew how that went. She'd stuck to Beau like glue, and he was beginning to think he wouldn't get to just shrug her off like he'd hoped.

"I know what it's like to struggle for something that might never happen." Beau spoke carefully. Weakness wasn't something he talked about if he could help it. "I also know what it's like to have someone take a chance on me only to have them turn around and virtually incinerate all my work."

"You're talking about VenTech?"

"Yes. When they bought my website ten years ago, they assured me they'd take it to the next level. Since they offered me more than it was worth, and I was eager to start another venture, I was hasty to accept. They didn't volunteer the fact that one of their private subsidiaries was an up-and-coming competitor of mine. They picked my work apart until it was a carcass."

"You came out on top, though. I read all about it. You got more out of that deal than you should've."

"If I hadn't sold it, my website would've destroyed the competition. George Wright, the founder, looked me in the eye and told me I could trust him, though."

Beau paused. He couldn't remember a time in the last ten years when he hadn't been tracking VenTech's stock, waiting for the company to stumble. "I guess back then, it wasn't all about the money." It felt more like an admission to himself than to the mayor. It'd been a while since his fortune hadn't sat in the number one spot on his list of priorities.

"So that's why you put on the conference?" Glenn asked. "To prevent others from making the same mistakes?"

Beau had his go-to response ready—he funded the convention because the young entrepreneurs of Los Angeles were America's tomorrow. But instead, he gave Churchill the real reason. "I never forgot how it felt when those bastards trashed years of blood, sweat and tears. Yes, I do it to provide entrepreneurs with the resources I didn't have, either because they don't know about them or can't afford them. Even though I came out on top in my deal, perhaps with proper legal help, I could've put that company on a better course."

Glenn nodded knowingly. "I understand. A man never gets the taste of his first real failure out of his mouth. Not with money, not with revenge." He frowned. "I'll be honest, I was reluctant to take this meeting. People are always coming to me with what I can do for them. Not what they can do for Los Angeles."

"I've always been upfront with you about the fact that I'm a businessman first, but entrepreneurial growth in Los Angeles benefits us all in the long term. And that starts with a conversation about tax reform."

"When you cut the bullshit, Olivier, you're all right. People like me, we see a lot of crap. Men putting me on, getting me a drink here and there, trying to shake my hand, hungry smiles, wives slobbering on men who aren't their husbands. It's a breath of fresh air to see this side of you. And I know where it's coming from."

"I'm sorry?"

"We've talked here and there at events. Seen you in the tabloids with women too. You're different with Lola."

Was he different? Or was Churchill under Lola's spell, the way Beau had been? Who was he kidding— Beau was still under her spell. He fought himself not to look at his watch. He hadn't forgotten that Lola might still be walking home.

Beau opened his mouth to tell Churchill he was right—Beau was a changed man, and it was all because of the amazing woman at his side. It wasn't exactly a lie. Beau *had* been different with her. "She's…"

Glenn tilted his head. "Yes?"

Beau could easily ignore everything they'd just discussed and take the easy route. But Churchill was a good guy who deserved the truth. "She's not too happy with me at the moment," Beau admitted. "We had an argument, and it's—well, things between us are—over."

"I see." Glenn took his mug by the handle but didn't drink. He just squinted at Beau. "I'm not all that surprised, actually. I don't mean this as an insult to you but a compliment to her—it would take a certain kind of man to hang on to a woman like that. Do you think you're that man?"

Beau had no doubt he was. If he wanted Lola as his own, for good, he could have her. There was no question about that—he'd done it once, and no matter how much work it would be, he could do it again. Beau was a better man than Johnny—and fuck, he was certainly a better man *for Lola* than Johnny.

"Yes," Beau said. "Lola and I are—" What did he want to say? Not that they were a perfect fit. Maybe that they were *both* hard to handle, *both* impossible to hang on to, but that if anyone could, it would be each other.

"Look," Churchill said. "Can I give you some advice? Don't be an idiot. Whatever you did, make it right. If Lola truly is like my wife, which I suspect she is, she needs someone who won't be deterred by anything. And those kinds of men are few and far between."

Beau hadn't been deterred by anything yet. Not Johnny, not Lola's resistance to his offer, not the fact that in order to win her love and win his game, he'd had to open up to her in a way he never had to anyone—not even Brigitte, who was like family.

Beau only focused on challenges that held a prize worthy of everything he had. He'd wanted his pride back. He'd wanted to redeem himself of the one failure he'd never overcome. But now it began to dawn on Beau—maybe he'd made the mistake of ignoring what was truly at stake. And maybe he'd been fighting for the wrong prize all along.

Chapter Five

The front door of Lola's apartment was unlocked, and she walked right in.

Johnny sprang instantly from the couch. "The sun's been up over an hour." He met her at the door, clasping her shoulders. "Are you all right?"

She looked into his earnest face. His concern was clear, but it was also overdue. Any number of things could've happened to Lola overnight. She could've been kidnapped by a crazy gunman and whisked away in a pricey sports car. She could've encountered a stilted admirer from ten years ago who'd never let go of his grudge. Considering whom she and Johnny were dealing with, being late at all was actually a perfectly valid cause for alarm.

"I'm fine," she said.

"I was worried. I thought about calling the cops."

"Did you?"

"Well…no." His eyebrows lowered. "What would I have told them?"

Maybe that she'd spent the night with the devil himself?

"I don't know," she said, wriggling out of his grip. The glass coffee table shook when she set the package of money on it. She stretched her aching arms and rolled her wrists. "We got into an argument. I refused a ride, so I walked."

"From where?"

"The hotel."

Johnny cocked his head. "He took you to a hotel? Doesn't he live in L.A.?"

Lola stared at him a moment. Johnny was a pretty big guy. He wasn't quite as tall as Beau, but he was meatier. *He* should've been the one to keep her safe in the gas station, but he hadn't even been there. She would've been there for Johnny. *She* never would've let him go off with a stranger. All so he could buy a fucking bar.

She was already heated from her walk. The more she'd thought about all the wrongs done to her by both men, the faster she'd strode and the higher her temper had risen. She knew what she had to do—what she *wanted* to do—but in all her anger, she hadn't stopped to figure this part out yet.

She turned away from Johnny, and her eyes landed on several days' worth of mail scattered on the counter. She'd start there. She walked over and sorted quickly through it, grabbing anything addressed to her.

"Was the hotel nearby at least?" Johnny asked.

"Beverly Hills."

"That's miles away."

She was well aware. She returned to the coffee table and dropped some envelopes next to the cash.

"I would've picked you up," Johnny said, following her from room to room. "You should've called."

She faced him, and her heart clenched. He could be so clueless. His simplicity was one of the things she loved about him except when she needed him to not be that. Like now, when what she was about to do would be that much harder because he had no idea it was coming.

She wrung her hands. "Johnny—"

He waited. "Yeah?"

Her heartbeat ping-ponged at the same rate as her thoughts. There was no right way to say *I care about you, but you screwed me over, but I don't want to hurt you, but I can't stay here anymore.* Was it fair that maybe some small part of her might *want* to hurt him for this? Did she even owe him an explanation? Had he just sat here on his ass all night, staring at a wall as she'd been bound, fucked, wooed, robbed, loved and then broken? Her chest stuttered with a deep breath, her fear ebbing slightly as anger took over again.

"I couldn't call you," she said. "My purse was stolen last night, and my phone was in it."

"Stolen? What the hell happened?" He let her pass to the bedroom. "Lola, for God's sake, stop moving around and talk to me."

She turned around. It was a plea, not an order, but she was tired of being told what to do. Just because

Johnny didn't do things the same way as Beau didn't mean he hadn't also treated her like a pawn. Not giving her a straight answer, forcing her to make the decision for both of them—that was how he'd manipulated her. She hadn't seen it clearly at the time, but now it was all she saw.

"Don't tell me what to do," she said, her eyes narrowed.

He pulled back a little. "What? I'm not. I just want you to slow down, and tell me what's going on."

"Why should I? Do you honestly care how my night went?"

He raised his eyebrows and scoffed in a way that sounded like a laugh—as though she'd made a joke. "Of course I care. What kind of a question is that? You're acting like—" He stopped. His neck reddened around the collar of his T-shirt. "Holy shit. Did you…did he give you something?"

Beau had given her lots of things. Almost as many as he'd taken. But she didn't think that was what Johnny meant. "Like what?"

"You're not yourself. You can't stand still, and you look at me like you don't recognize me. No matter how long it's been, I haven't forgotten how you get when you're high."

Her mouth fell open. *High?* She wasn't high. She was pissed. Johnny *would* jump to that conclusion at the first sign of her old self. Spending two nights with Beau had reminded her of the girl she used to be. As Beau had embraced that about her, it became clearer that Johnny never had. He didn't like her wild.

38

The accusation was so offensive, she couldn't even deny it. The man she loved acted as though he didn't even know her. If she'd changed over the years, maybe he had too. Or maybe it was that she'd cared so fiercely about him, was so grateful to him, that she hadn't seen the truth. He wasn't etched into her heart, woven into her soul. She didn't feel him in her every movement—it wasn't *his* love that coursed through her veins like blood.

She went to the hallway closet and slid a cardboard box from the top shelf.

"What're you doing?" he asked.

She crouched, lifted the lid and fingered through some folders until she found one labeled *Important Papers—Lola*. She took it, along with her passport and a credit card she'd filed away earlier that year when she and Johnny had opened a joint account.

"Did you hear me?" he persisted. "I asked what the fuck you're on."

She stood up. The papers rustled as she clutched them. "I'm not high, and you have no right to ask me that."

"I have every right. It's the only explanation. It's just like those nights you used to come into Hey Joe after an especially rough shift."

Her mouth tingled, bitterness on her tongue. She'd barely been an adult back then—she'd fucked up just like every other teenager. Why was she paying for those mistakes now? Everything in her body was tight, and if he kept plucking at her, she would snap.

"Look at you—you're shaking," Johnny said. "Your eyes are watering, your hair's a mess—"

"My eyes are watering from lack of sleep and because cars have been kicking dirt into my face for the last hour. I'm shaking because I just carried five hundred thousand dollars over two miles."

"If I'd known, I would've picked you up. I told you that. Don't take it out on me."

As if he hadn't played a role in any of this. As if her anger was completely out of left field. "Fuck you, Johnny. Just fuck you."

His eyes doubled in size. "Fuck *me*? Why?"

"You know why." She continued to their room and grabbed a duffel bag from the closet.

"You come in here like a tornado, get me all worked up and say fuck *me*?"

"You used me. Both of you." She was practically shuddering now. "Everybody got what they wanted, even me, but at what price?"

Johnny threw both hands in the air. "Seriously, what the fuck? That's completely unfair. We made every decision together."

"*I* made every decision. By myself. *I* had to decide how much money I was worth."

"Bullshit. We both knew it was just an exchange. It was never about what you were worth. I didn't ask you to do this."

"You didn't ask me not to." She ripped articles of clothing off their hangers and stuffed them into the bag. "What choice did I have? If I'd said no, you would've always resented me for the life we could've had. I did this for us."

"And you didn't enjoy it at all, did you?" His lips compressed into a line. "You practically jumped at the chance do it again."

Her throat closed. He wasn't wrong—she'd been clinging to the lie that she hadn't wanted to go back to Beau. What did that make her? What did that make Johnny? If he'd even suspected she'd wanted this and he still hadn't stopped her, then he'd gambled with her.

"Just admit that you liked it," he said. "A million-dollar price tag made you feel pretty damn special."

"*Special?*" She could barely get the word out, her head burning like her entire body was on fire. She slammed her fists on the bed. "You think having two men use me to boost their egos is *special?* I have a stranger's cum on my pants and more money than I know what to do with. Does that make me *special?*"

"Jesus Christ." Johnny staggered back. "Like I need that fucking mental image."

"Yeah?" She grabbed a stack of his jeans from a shelf and threw them on the ground. "Well, at least you didn't live through it!"

"I did live through it," he said. "Except I had to use my imagination. All the things he was getting for his money. Tell me what they were, Lola. Why you? What did you give him that someone else couldn't?"

She shook her head. He had no idea the mental images she could give him—like the one where Beau had *seduced* her in to fucking him every which way while he plotted how to hurt her the most. "You don't know what you're asking for. You can't handle details."

"Try me."

"I know you, Johnny. Just let it go. It's not worth—"

"I can handle it," he said, raising his voice. "What was he like? Was it better? What did you let him do?"

Lola's body tightened at just the threat of a memory. As if she'd had any control over what Beau did to her. Once the sun went down, her body had become his. It'd breathed for him, thrummed for him, come for him. And he'd been thorough with each inch of her, leaving no part untouched.

"Everything," she said levelly.

He shook his head hard. "I don't believe you."

"Everything one man can do to one woman, he did to me. My mouth, my pussy, my ass. He had it all."

"You let him—?" Johnny reached back, grasping at nothing. "But you never…you wouldn't—for years I've asked you for that. He got it in two nights?"

"That's what you *sold* him. Don't act like you didn't know. You were there for the negotiation."

"And you promised me you were safe—that he didn't force you into anything."

She'd protected Johnny too long. No matter what he thought, he hadn't lived through what she had. He had to accept his share of the blame for everything that'd happened the last few weeks. "He didn't take a thing, Johnny. He waited for me to come to him, and I did. I gave him what he wanted."

"Liar," he said. "You can enjoy it, but you can't want it. That's not fair."

"It wasn't just sex for me. It was more."

Johnny pointed at the duffel bag. "Is that what this is about? You're going to see him again?"

"No. This is about you and me." While Beau might've been the catalyst behind their breakup, he wasn't the reason. He had his own sins to pay for, but she couldn't blame him for this. "I'm not the girl you want. I tried so hard, I honestly thought I was all these years. But I need more. I don't want to spend my life doing something mediocre, like working at Hey Joe. It doesn't make me happy."

"Mediocre?" he repeated. "Oh. I see. One night with a millionaire and suddenly you're too good for me. That's just bullshit." He picked her bag up off the bed and held it to his side. "I know you're angry. So am I. But stop and think about what you're saying."

Lola tried to take the bag. "We're finished—"

"No." He pulled the duffel back and went to block the doorway. "You don't just fall out of love overnight because you slept with someone else."

"I already told you, this isn't about him. You fucked up, and because of that, I see the truth. What we have is easy. I love and care about you, Johnny, but I'm not in love with you." She tried to get by him, but he stayed where he was. "Give me my bag. I'm leaving."

He visibly tried to speak, but nothing came. He opened and closed his free hand as if grasping for something.

43

"Johnny. *Move.*" She shoved him aside, and he dropped the bag to grab her wrists. They struggled for a second and then both stopped, their breathing labored. Neither of them moved as they stared at each other.

He released her. "Don't do this."

She hoisted the bag off the ground and walked down the hallway.

"Amanda blew me in the stockroom," he yelled. "I guess that means I fell out of love with you too. Is that how it works?"

Lola's heart dropped. Her hand went automatically to her stomach as she turned around. "Amanda?"

He ran a hand over his hair, also looking like he might be sick. "Doesn't feel so good, does it?"

Lola could've smacked the pathetic, somehow smug, look off his paling face. She hadn't thought him capable of cheating, but the last few weeks, he'd been a different person. A weaker one. It didn't surprise her as much as it should've.

"When?"

"Last night."

"You piece of shit."

He shrugged, but he looked anything but casual. "I needed someone, and she was there."

Lola's eyebrows weighed heavy. She was too livid to feel hurt. "And where was I?" she asked. "Screwing another man to give you *your* dream."

"Oh, don't fucking kid yourself. You're the only one who gets to have a little fun on the side?" His face fell. He walked toward her, but she backed away. "I drank a handle trying to forget what you were doing. It didn't even put a dent in me, Lo. I tried to stop her. I pushed her away. It meant nothing."

It meant everything—a permanent nail in their coffin. "It's not nothing to me. You gave me away twice, and now you sealed your fate. What if I'd come home, and we'd moved on with our lives? Did you think I could forgive this?"

"Yes, because it was all I had. I was desperate. I've never been as miserable as I was last night."

"Poor fucking baby." She scoffed. "I can't believe Beau was right about you."

"About me?" He touched his chest. "What did he tell you?"

"He said resentment makes people do ugly things—like cheat on their loved ones. He said you'd do that."

"That's rich coming from him of all people," Johnny said. "You let him talk about me that way?"

"You don't seem to understand," Lola said evenly. "I don't let him do or not do anything. He *does* and *says* what he wants. Did I think he was completely crazy for saying that? Yes. But apparently I was the crazy one for thinking I could trust you."

"This is such bullshit. And I was supposed to trust you after finding out you actually enjoyed sleeping with someone else? By my count, I'd say we're about even."

Her jaw tingled. She was disgusted with the whole thing—Johnny and that desperate slut. "Asshole. Did you stick your dick anywhere other than her mouth last night?"

"No."

"Did you finish? Come all over her? I bet she just gobbled it up. How many times have you done this behind my back?"

"Never. You know me better than that."

"I don't know anything or anyone anymore." She turned and left the hallway. "You can all go to hell."

"Where are you going?"

She had no idea. She just had to get out of there as soon as possible. She transferred everything from the coffee table into her bag. "I'm taking my half of the money."

"Lola, come on. Don't do this. I'll go to Mark's and give you some space to cool off. We'll figure this out when we both calm down."

She looked over her shoulder at him. "You know it's over. Don't act like I'm the only reason we're through. You had to have known at some point this could happen."

"I didn't. I swear. Did you?"

She bit the inside of her cheek. He could only be that oblivious if he was shrouded in denial. "Yes," she admitted.

"When? Did you know this could end us before you left the apartment last night?"

She turned to face him completely. For nine years, she'd believed Johnny was the one. She would've married him if he'd asked. She'd wanted his children. She'd convinced herself that what she'd done for him— maturing, settling down—was something everyone did at some point. It was hard to believe that not only had she not questioned that, but that it'd only taken her two nights with Beau to wake up.

She'd been blind to her needs and feelings too long, but she was paying attention now. That part of her life was over, and in this next part, she'd be putting one person first—herself. She wasn't sure where she was going or what she wanted, but it would be on her terms.

When had she known it was over with Johnny? Perhaps it was when she'd sat in Beau's lap and told him she loved him, the words falling out of her mouth, slippery and dangerous. Maybe it'd been even earlier than that, when she'd made that phone call to Beau in the middle of the night, or when she'd gotten into his limo the second time. But when had it all started?

"I knew we were in trouble when I realized you were considering Beau's offer. I trusted you a little less. I need to know I'm more important to the man I'm with than anything else."

"But you are the most important thing," he said. "I love you."

Lola went to the kitchen. She found the package of cash Beau'd left on the counter the night before. It was unopened with her and Johnny's camping picture still sitting on top. She dumped it into her bag with the rest of the million dollars. She left the photo. She left the apartment. She didn't stop to check if Johnny was all right—because she left that part of herself behind too.

Chapter Six

Beau rolled his neck until he got a satisfying crack. The elevator beeped with each floor it passed, the digital numbers ticking down. It'd been a long day of slicing through the usual bullshit red tape that came with his line of work. He counted his meeting with Churchill a success, and he'd put out a fire at work while simultaneously closing a deal, but his duties weren't over yet. His assistant had sent him back to the hotel at four to change for some event tonight, one he didn't even remember committing to. He'd lost track of how many hours had passed since he'd slept. Over twenty-four. Lola had been gone around twelve. He was lucky to be standing.

The doors split apart. He exited, turned the corner on his way to meet Brigitte and ran right into Heather the concierge. She dropped a folder of papers that scattered on the lobby floor.

"Oh, shit," she said, crouching. "I'm so sorry."

Beau also squatted to help her as people passed around them. "My fault. I wasn't watching. Where are you off to in such a rush?"

She smiled at the floor. "As soon as I get these to the back office, I'm done for the night. I worked a double shift. I need a drink."

"I see." Beau glanced up and handed her the papers he'd gathered. He could guess what was coming.

"I was just going to grab one here if you're interested," she said, pointing in the direction of the lounge.

Blowing off whatever event he was going to didn't sound like such a bad idea, but Brigitte and Warner were waiting out front. "I have somewhere to be, and I won't be back until after ten." He stood, brushing off his pants. "I should get going, actually."

"Well," Heather said as she also rose, running a hand through her hair, "that's only a few hours. I don't mind waiting—"

Beau did a double take at the mirror over Heather's shoulder. In the reflection, just as the elevator behind him closed, he caught a flash of dark hair, a stark-white dress. His gut lurched—*Lola*. He jerked around a second too late. The doors had shut.

He blinked. It couldn't have been her. It didn't make sense. Lola had no reason to be at that hotel unless it was to see Beau, and in order to get to the elevator, she would've walked right by him.

Beau blinked and looked back at Heather. "You said you've been at the front desk all day?"

She nodded earnestly.

"Did a woman named Lola check in? Black hair, blue eyes."

Heather grinned and swatted his arm. "Do you have any idea how many people come through this lobby a day? I couldn't possibly remember—"

"Try," he said. "Lola Winters. It's important."

Her smile fell. "Um. Doesn't sound familiar?"

Beau looked behind him and stared at the elevator, willing the doors to reopen. The numbers above it rose until stopping at eleven. He waited. After a brief pause, they began counting down again. If she were there to see him, she would've gone to Beau's room, which was on the sixteenth floor.

Beau rubbed his eyes. All day, they'd been burning with fatigue. He needed sleep, and that was the only explanation for his confusion. He hadn't even napped, not that he would've if he had the time. The last time he'd taken a nap was between shifts when he was in his twenties—and he was no longer that kid. He'd made damn well sure of it.

"Mr. Olivier?"

He looked at Heather. "What?"

"I asked if you'd like me to go see about your friend."

"Oh. No." He checked his watch. "I don't know what I was thinking. I've got to run."

"What about the drink?"

"Can't." Beau stepped around her. "Night, Heather."

Out front, Brigitte leaned against Warner's town car in a short, red dress. Through the dusk, a tiny orange light buzzed around her like a fly. For all intents and purposes, Brigitte was his sister, more family to him than his own mother. For that reason, her risqué attire had no effect on him, but Beau wasn't sure the same could be said for Warner. He didn't even notice Beau walking in their direction.

As soon as she spotted Beau, her back straightened. "There you are." Her French accent made it sound less accusatory. "I've been trying to reach you all day."

Beau silently thanked his assistant for keeping Brigitte at bay all day. "My phone is in pieces. I had to get a new one."

"Oh. Sounds positively sordid. I want all the details from last night."

"I'm not in the mood, Brigitte."

She arched a thin, manicured—and angry—eyebrow. "Not in the mood?" she repeated. "Ten years you've been sulking over this woman who fucked you over. And now that you've gotten your revenge, you're not in the mood to share? I thought you'd be bursting at the seams."

"I'm not." He eyed Warner. "Thanks for keeping her company."

"My pleasure, sir. Good evening."

"We're headed to the Los Angeles Athletic Club for an event."

"Yes, sir." Warner leaned over Brigitte to get the door for her.

She touched his cheek, smiling. *"Merci, mon chéri."*

Warner simply nodded, but there was no mistaking the red tint of his face.

Beau waited until Warner'd returned to the front of the car to look back at Brigitte. "I don't care that you're a merciless flirt, but does it have to be with my employee?"

She took a deep drag of her cigarette and waved him off. "You're grumpy."

Beau took it out of her hand and tossed it on the ground. "You'll smell like smoke all night," he said, mashing it with his shoe.

"Everyone smokes in Europe."

Beau got into the car, grumbling, "We aren't in Europe."

She followed him into the backseat. "I looked up the guest list for tonight's event, and it's primarily Europeans. There're potential investors around every corner. You know that."

"I see. And the smoking is so you'll fit in?"

"I don't need to tell you people's wallets loosen when they're more comfortable."

"All right. Do what you like." Beau turned to the window. The woman on the elevator had jolted him. It was a split-second glimpse, but he'd been sure. He didn't trust his gut with Lola, though, not after the last few weeks, not when he was this tired. She had no reason to come back to him and no business on the eleventh floor.

He'd been trying not to think of her, but her name had been phantom-like on his mind all day, like a number he was trying to remember for later. She'd disappeared, clean and quick. There one second, gone the next. According to plan. There'd be no stuff of breakups—late night calls, pleas to reconsider, checking in on someone you cared about.

Beau sat forward, the leather creaking. Even if he wanted to, he couldn't drop by Hey Joe or her apartment or even call her. She wouldn't be there. Her purse had been stolen—credit cards, phone and all.

"Beau."

Startled by Brigitte's sharp tone, he turned back to her. "What?"

"What happened last night? You're completely out of it."

Fatigue was setting in. Beau wasn't in his twenties anymore, and while he wouldn't have taken back any of his time with Lola, pulling two all-nighters in the same month was taking its toll. "I could give a shit about these parties. We went to a fundraiser on Monday. I have a gala to attend tomorrow night. Why?"

She put her hand over his. "You know this comes with the territory. It's never bothered you before."

He set an elbow on the armrest, massaged the bridge of his nose. "Maybe it has, and I just never told you."

"Nonsense. We're a team. We've been at this for years, networking. Don't tell me it doesn't pay off."

Beau wanted his hand back to check his phone. He normally took time in the backseat to catch up on work, but if Brigitte lost any of his attention, she would only work harder to get it back.

"Sometimes it's too much," he said.

She sucked in her cheeks just a little, tightening her grip on his hand. "What's too much?"

People were always trying to get to Beau. With wealth, things fell in his lap—opportunities for him to get in at the ground level, to make a killing, to fuck up. The carousel never ended. It was supposed to be a good thing, but Beau was rarely cavalier with anything, and everything required research. It could get exhausting. Brigitte wasn't the only one vying for his attention. There was no way to put it into words without sounding ungrateful, so he shook his head. "Never mind."

Brigitte was quiet a moment, and he was thankful for the reprieve. Her fingers were still curled tightly around his hand. "You didn't go through with it."

He stared out the window. "Yes, I did."

"I don't believe you. You didn't break things off, and that's why you don't want to go tonight. You're just waiting to get back to her. Where is she? In the room?"

"I told you, it's done."

"Then why are you acting like this? We're supposed to be celebrating our victory, not sulking."

He looked back at her. "*Our* victory?"

Brigitte reeled away. "I've been there every step of the way, haven't I? You were my rock when our parents died, and you make it so hard for me to repay you for that."

"Nobody's keeping score. You don't owe me anything."

"I do it because I *want* to. I never would've gotten through my mom's death alone. When someone hurts you, they hurt me too. I lived your pain when she undid all your hard work and ruined everything. Last night was redemption for both of us."

"You didn't do any of the dirty work, though. You didn't see her face." Beau could. He could see it right then—her mouth, normally hard, had finally become delicate with him. She'd hated him that first night, and he'd gotten her to love him by the end. Her hard-won delicate mouth, mangled with disgust when he'd told her the truth. The immediate reversal of everything he'd worked for. The way she'd flinched, recoiled, when he'd tried to touch her. He'd thought, if he could just get her in his arms, he could make her see.

"Describe it to me," Brigitte said. "I want to know it all."

He blinked at her. "Did you mean for her to see that text?"

Brigitte loosened her fingers, tapped them giddily over his knuckles. "You mean this morning? Why? Did she?"

"It doesn't matter. It's all over—me and her, her and Johnny."

"Really?" Brigitte asked, her tone pitchy. "Here I was worried you'd chickened out, but I should've known—you never do anything halfway."

He angled his head at her, knowing he should let it go. "Excuse me?"

"She and Johnny are over—why?" She paused only a second. "Because she chose you, right? You're the center of her world. She loves you. But she also hates you. You did more than break her heart—you grabbed her by it, pulled her inside out. You put her life on a completely different course. That's power, Beau."

It was a cold truth, one that would sicken anyone else. Not Beau, though. Lola's world revolving around him made him feel good. Wherever she was, she was thinking of him, and her thoughts weren't casual. They weren't nothing.

"Or maybe I'm wrong," Brigitte said, throwing the words out like a fishing line in a pond.

He bit. "Why?"

She studied him. "You're on her mind, there's no question, but she's also on yours. It would appear after all you've done to overcome it, she still has some power over you."

The car stopped at a light, turning the backseat tomato-red. The engine hummed. "Nobody has power over me," Beau said evenly. "Not even you."

Brigitte leaned over to stroke the back of Beau's hair. Her arm reeked of cigarettes. "You're frustrated, and I know why. It has nothing to do with her."

Beau sighed deeply, pointedly not asking why. He considered telling Warner to turn the car around so he could end this day already.

"You miss the thrill of conquest," Brigitte continued. "For weeks, you had this singular goal to focus on. Now that it's over, you don't know what to do with all this nervous energy. Trust me, it isn't Lola you want."

"I suppose you know what I want."

"Of course I do." She smiled. "We need a new challenge."

"There's no *we*, Brigitte. Any mistakes I've made are mine alone. This was my game."

Brigitte returned to her side of the car. "Mistakes?"

The glasses of the built-in bar rattled as they turned a corner. He'd meant to say conquests, not mistakes, but maybe that's what this had all been. One big mistake. "Yes."

"Don't you dare insult me by saying that whore means anything to you," Brigitte said. "I'm the one who *saved* you from making a mistake—twice."

"Calm down. You're getting hysterical."

"You called and woke me up last night to tell me you didn't think you could go through with it. I talked you off the ledge. Obviously, I didn't know if she'd see my text this morning, but I knew you would—and I knew you'd regret it if at any point in the night, you got off course."

"You don't know shit. You weren't there. You didn't see what I did."

"Jesus, the woman makes a fool of you over and over. It's disgusting."

Beau pitied his sister. She wanted so desperately to be a part of something, to belong, that she resorted to grasping at straws. Anything to get under Beau's skin. He wondered if there would ever come a time she didn't want to be there.

"That's enough."

"It's sad to see you think you're in charge when she is. Even I have more control—"

"Enough," he snapped.

"What are you going to do? Spank me? Is that what you did to her when she said something you didn't like?"

Beau's nostrils flared with a sharp inhalation. He could still picture the red curve of Lola's ass after he'd smacked it. He hadn't held back in the least, but she'd taken everything without complaint. If he wanted to do it again, why shouldn't he? There was no woman out there who'd walk away from him if he put his mind to getting her in his bed—including Lola.

Brigitte rolled her eyes. "Just like every other pathetic idiot who's charmed by a decent pair of tits."

He grabbed her bicep and pulled her across the backseat. "I'd watch my mouth if I were you. Nobody talks to me that way."

The car jolted as Warner hit the brakes. "Sir," he said, glancing at them in the rearview mirror.

"Stay out of this, Warner. Brigitte knows exactly what she's doing."

"What am I doing?" she asked, blinking at him. "You're my brother, and I love you. All I want is for you to be happy. Believe me, she won't make you happy."

"You only want me to be happy if it means I'm alone. You're worried if I find someone else, you'll lose me."

"Someone else?" Brigitte's eyes twinkled. "Surely you don't mean Lola? Come on. Deep down you know the truth."

Beau restrained from flinging her away. She would say anything to needle him, and she couldn't possibly know what the truth was. She hadn't spent more than ten minutes in the same room as Lola and Beau. But he spat the words, unable to help himself. "What's the truth?"

"You'll never have her. Do you honestly believe after what you've done, you could get her back?" Brigitte sniffed. "Your money didn't matter to her then, and it means even less now. You can't buy her, and that's the only way you know how to get anything."

"Bullshit. I went twenty-seven years before I ever made a dime."

"Exactly, and not even Warner would've looked in your direction before your money. You had nothing and no one."

"Brigitte," Warner cautioned from the front seat.

She ignored him. "No one except me."

Beau's temper was getting the best of him. "Brigitte, I'm about as patient with you as can be most of the time, but you're pressing the wrong buttons."

"You have no way of winning Lola back. You'll never be what she needs."

Beau pushed her off. "You don't know what you're talking about."

"She's better off without you."

Beau set his jaw and stared forward at nothing. He didn't have to look at her to know she wore a smug expression. "Put some perfume on. You fucking stink."

What pissed Beau off the most was that Brigitte was right. Lola was better off without the man she'd met in front of Hey Joe, but Beau didn't feel like that man anymore. If Lola hadn't left that morning, if she hadn't seen that text, Beau would've taken care of her in ways Johnny never could've. That had to count for

something. And if he wanted her back, nothing would
get in his way.

Chapter Seven

They'd circled her neighborhood twice already, Lola biting her nails, the cab driver growing impatient. "Come on, lady, where you want to go?" he kept asking.

Walking out on Johnny had sounded easier when she'd known Warner would be out front, waiting to drive her back to Beau at the Four Seasons. For a little while, she'd had two homes, and now, she didn't even have one.

They hadn't had a real relationship in a while, but Lola could've shown up at her mom's house without an explanation. The place she'd grown up had stopped being home a long time ago, though, and she hadn't gone crawling back yet. Her mom might not say "I told you so," but she'd be thinking it, the words close to the surface even eleven years after Lola'd moved out to strip.

She put her hand on the black duffel bag and felt the money just underneath the fabric. She had little of her own, but what she did have was hers without a doubt. An inordinate amount of cash. A freedom most people couldn't dream of. The chance to leave her troubles behind. There were things at the apartment she might've liked to keep—mostly photos or mementos—but everything she needed was there on the seat next to her. She no longer had anything tying her to Los Angeles.

Beau had cut deep, though. In two nights, he'd seen inside her, and like she'd told him in the shower—she'd felt him there like a thunderstorm. On her stomach, on his hotel bed, he'd had her at her most vulnerable, but it was more than physical. She'd trusted him. And in return, he'd treated her like one of his companies, an investment, a challenge, leading her down a path painstakingly designed to get her where he wanted.

How many people had fallen prey to his charms, been the subject of his fascination, been manipulated by him? She had no idea, but she knew this—Beau had never paid the price for his sins. Nobody'd ever had the weapons to use against him, and he'd made sure of that. Every careful step Beau made in his life was toward wealth, but Lola knew it wasn't the money he cared about. It was the power it afforded him. While his bank account was fat, nobody could ever deny him anything.

Lola felt it like a knot in her chest, the indignity of it. Beau couldn't be allowed to play with people's lives anymore. He deserved to feel her pain as if it were his own. He'd once said to her that a man of his wealth trusted his enemies more than his friends. Lola was an enemy now, but she'd been a friend to him once, and she could be that again.

Lola looked at the driver in the rearview mirror. "Take me to Rodeo Drive."

If she was going to play Beau's game, she had to look the part—and that meant buying herself a wardrobe fit for the queen Beau had once believed her to be.

◆ ◆ ◆

Lola stepped out of the cab and looked up at the towering Four Seasons. With a garment bag draped across her arm and a million dollars slung over her shoulder, she entered the hotel. She wore her new white dress, a form-fitting, short little thing she never would've looked twice at before. She was greeted by three different men before she reached the front desk.

"Good evening." The male concierge smiled. "How can I help you?"

Lola handed him her passport, currently her only form of identification. "I need a room."

He dropped his eyes to the computer. After a few clicks of his mouse, he nodded. "You're in luck. We have a couple left. How many nights?"

Lola traced her finger over the marble counter. She had to act fast. Beau was a man of resolve, but she meant something to him. He'd be confused by that, his memories and wounds fresh, his need for revenge less pressing than he'd thought. She needed to worm her way back in before he'd hardened into something unbreakable again. "One night. And I'm paying in cash."

"That's fine," he said. "I'll need a card for incidentals, though."

Lola hesitated. She had no plan yet, and she preferred to stay off the grid until she knew more. "You won't charge it?"

"Not unless you give us a reason to. There will be a pending charge, but it'll fall off after a day or two."

She gave it over reluctantly, leaving her hand open for the few seconds it took the concierge to swipe it. He handed it back to her and slid a keycard across the counter. "How's the eleventh floor?"

"Fine."

"Do you need assistance to your room?"

She shrugged a shoulder and showed him her bags. "This is everything I own."

He glanced over the counter and raised his eyebrows. "Not much, is it?"

A voice behind her stopped Lola's response in her throat. She would've recognized it anywhere, from the gates of heaven to the depths of hell and everywhere in between.

Her heart pounded. The concierge spoke, but she couldn't hear him. Five minutes in the lobby, and she was already going to see Beau again. She hadn't planned for it, but she hadn't planned for anything yet. Her only goal was to reconcile with him as quickly as she could.

She inhaled a deep breath to calm herself. Beau would sense any fear and trepidation in an instant. She picked up the key from the counter and turned around. Beau was squatted on the floor next to a pretty blonde.

She didn't wait to find out why. She seized the chance to pass him while his head was down. This wasn't the right time to see him. She needed time to figure out some kind of strategy.

"There's always a plan, Lola."

Lola punched the "Up" button, thankful the elevator was already there. Inside, she selected the eleventh floor and tried to turn away. She couldn't. She watched in a nearby mirror as he stood. It was almost reassuring to see him again. It was clear as day to her now, how she'd associated being near him with safety. The feeling passed quickly, and she concentrated instead on grasping tidbits of his conversation with the girl.

"…somewhere to be…after ten."

"…only a few hours. I don't mind waiting…"

The doors began to close, and as they met in the middle, Beau's eyes shifted over. Her breath caught. A second passed, and the elevator rose with a jolt. Even if he'd seen her, she didn't think it'd been enough time to recognize her. Still, with every floor she passed, tension gripped her, and it didn't let go until she was safe in her room.

She dumped her things on the cloudlike comforter and went directly to change the temperature. Johnny had always kept the thermostat low, complaining about the heat even on the mildest Los Angeles nights. The men in Lola's life were oversized children who'd chosen themselves over her time and time again. And yet they always seemed to come out on top—Johnny had half her money and a new plaything. Beau had blonde girls at his feet. Her dad was off somewhere, not taking care of anyone, the way he liked it.

Lola got to her knees and opened the minibar. She downed three bottles of liquor, one right after another, making a mental note to pay for them later in cash. Who did *she* have? Herself. She wasn't an abandoned daughter. She wasn't Johnny's girlfriend or Beau's conquest. Nobody would tell her where she was going or how to get there anymore. She wouldn't give them that control. She drank three more bottles and crawled over to the hotel phone. She picked up the receiver and angrily punched in the number for Hey Joe.

Johnny answered. "Hello?"

"You weren't supposed to cheat. Ever. But why her? She wasn't even a blip on my radar."

"I—"

"I don't even care," Lola said. "That's bad, isn't it? He hurt me more. I'm sorry if that makes you sad. I saw him with a woman today, a fucking blonde."

"I think you have the wrong number."

"I thought he liked brunettes." She frowned, her mind playing catch up. "What? Is this Hey Joe?"

"No. You called a home number."

Lola hung up and lay on the carpet. Life hadn't been that fair to her, but she didn't remember ever feeling like this. To still be so deeply in love with someone who'd gone out of his way to hurt her was more than one person should have to handle. She thought she should cry—it seemed like a healthy reaction. Nothing came. She stared up at the ceiling, forcing her eyes to stay open until they watered, until one salty drop slid from the corner of her eye to the edge of her lip. She wondered how much she'd have to drink for her tears to taste like vodka.

The sun set, painting the room orange. It was vivid and majestic, different from any sunset she'd ever seen. Or maybe it just seemed that way from upside down, drunk, eleven stories above the city.

She groaned. It wasn't enough, but she couldn't seem to move from that spot to get more alcohol. She closed her eyes, and the sunset streaked neon against the backs of her lids. Her hands and armpits were clammy, the hair at her temples damp with sweat.

Who was she to be angry with Johnny, though? He didn't even know the depth of her sins. *Her sins*— fucking the enemy and enjoying it. Letting the enemy close enough to break her heart. Loving the enemy.

Beau had a soft side. She already missed that. She even missed his hardness. Despite all the reasons not to, she'd come to trust him. Only a monster could invent a scheme to hurt someone so thoroughly. Only the devil himself would actually go through with it, though.

Beau's room was only five floors up from Lola's. She would've requested a room above his, but it seemed he was always at the top. The devil shouldn't get to live at the top, hiding in plain sight, moving people like pawns. The devil should have to suffer—just as his victims had.

Chapter Eight

Beau shut his eyes in the backseat of Warner's town car and pulled his necktie loose. The dinner conversation at tonight's event had dragged more than usual. Bids for his attention had been pushier too. In those situations, he was grateful to have Brigitte by his side. Unfazed by their earlier argument, she'd been her charming self all night.

"How'd it go?" Warner asked from the driver's seat.

Beau opened his eyes and blinked off sleep. It wasn't like Warner to chat, so it took him a minute to figure out if he'd dreamed it. He sat up a little. "What?"

"The event. Was Brigitte okay? I was afraid you might snap earlier."

"Oh." Beau nodded a little. "She's fine. She was great, actually. Nothing puts her in a better mood than getting me riled up."

"It's because she cares."

"All right." Beau didn't know what else to say. It wasn't really Warner's business, except that it was, because he was always there, observing. Beau just wanted to sleep, but Warner was glancing at him in the rearview mirror like the conversation wasn't over. "It's good for business anyway," he added.

"What is?"

"Brigitte, when she's happy. She's my secret weapon."

Warner grinned, a rare sight. He seemed satisfied with that and looked back out the windshield.

These events were prime hunting grounds. Old, rich men were weak for Brigitte's candid, often crude remarks—always delivered in a French accent. When Beau needed capital for one of his companies, he and Brigitte were a team that was hard to refuse. Usually.

Tonight, she'd dropped off buttered-up men at Beau's feet and strutted around like a lion after a fresh kill. Beau, on the other hand, had been distracted. He'd mixed up two of his companies and called an important man by the wrong name. There were things on his mind, though—like the woman he'd glimpsed in the reflection earlier.

Once, before they'd sat down to dinner, Beau had caught himself looking around the room for Lola, ridiculous as it was. She could be anywhere, though, including right there in that room. He still had no idea what'd happened to her once she'd walked off hotel property, and it was making him more and more agitated.

Warner turned the car into the Four Seasons' circular driveway and stopped to let him out. Beau reached for the door handle.

"I know you doubt yourself, but you're good to her," Warner said.

Beau looked to the front of the car. "Lola?"

"Brigitte." Warner frowned, his forehead wrinkling. "You're more patient than you think. She just loves having your attention."

Beau hesitated, somewhat embarrassed he'd thought Warner was talking about Lola. "Right. Well. It's been a long day—"

"Goodnight, sir."

"Yes. Goodnight." Beau shut the car door behind him and looked up. The hotel glowed, the lobby and the rooms, like it was filled with gold. Was Lola up there? Or was she just—gone? Walking inside was like trudging through mud. He was shutting down, his body crashing without enough sleep. He was almost to the elevator when he heard, "Mr. Olivier?"

Beau stopped, turning to the man at the front desk. "Yes?"

"Your visitor's in the lounge."

Beau was already removing his cufflinks, sticking them in his pockets. "You're mistaken. I'm not expecting anyone."

"She's been in there half an hour. She was very clear that you'd be expecting her and that she'd wait as long as necessary."

Beau squinted in the direction of the hotel bar, then glanced at his watch. It was 10:32 P.M., half an hour after he'd told Heather he'd be back. She'd be an easy fuck, requiring little to no effort on his part—just what he'd thought he needed. Sleep sounded more appealing.

"Do me a favor? Tell her I'm not interested and that I've gone to bed."

"I understand, sir." He cleared his throat. "She'll find someone who is. Half the staff is enamored by her."

Beau had turned toward the elevator again, but he stopped. There was no reason someone shouldn't be enamored by Heather—after all, she had tits for days, perky too, always a plus. But it made him think of Lola, sitting at a bar, single for the first time in almost a decade. No man in his right mind wouldn't be enamored by her, that was for certain.

It could only be Heather waiting for him. It had to be. Yet Beau found himself turning back and heading for the lounge. He wasn't one to ignore his instinct, and it told him it wasn't Heather he'd find in there—but the woman who'd been firmly entrenched in his thoughts since she'd walked out of his life that morning.

Chapter Nine

Present day

It wasn't even noon, and Lola had already charged seventeen hundred dollars to Beau's credit card. She hadn't lied to him in his foyer earlier that morning— each task on her to-do list was important, including shopping. In only weeks, she was becoming a reluctant regular on Rodeo Drive.

Beau worked long hours. Most days she met him for lunch, keeping herself fresh in his mind, but he rarely had more than a half hour to spare. So she would go to the park or to a museum or a matinee, and when she'd exhausted all those venues, Rodeo Drive welcomed her like an old friend—as long as she was carrying Beau's black American Express.

The Burberry trench coat in her shopping bag fit her like a second skin. All designer clothing was smooth that way. Easy to wear, easy to move in. If it wasn't, though, Beau's tailor would come to the house, take it away and return it to her better. But this particular coat wasn't for her. She wouldn't wear it to feel good or to exhibit wealth. She'd wear it for Beau—to make *him* feel good. That was the power of a well-made piece of clothing. Even though she only needed it for one night, if she bought herself anything less than the best, it would raise questions from him—and she didn't need questions she couldn't answer. She was playing a role in Beau's life, and that role was expensive.

Only three blocks constituted the main part of one the world's most expensive shopping streets. She walked over plaques honoring fashion icons and under California's signature palm trees, stopping in front of a high-end lingerie shop she'd been eyeing for a while.

She pulled open the glass door and descended black marble steps. Her heartbeat picked up a little. She might've been a woman just looking for something to please her man—or she might've been a woman experiencing her fantasy, three weeks in the making, coming to life.

A lady with a pinched smile approached her. "Good afternoon. What are you shopping for today?"

"Lingerie."

"What kind?"

Lola touched a white silk negligee and let it slide over her palms. "The kind that does the most damage."

The saleswoman made a noise. "I think that depends on the person wearing it."

Lola turned around to see her smile had turned genuine. Before Lola could answer, a flash of light near the window caught her eye. She crossed the small store and picked up a black, lace corset that sparkled when the sun hit it.

The garment was embedded with hundreds of tiny, glistening gemstones. "They're Swarovski crystals," the saleswoman said.

Of course they were. In Beau's hotel room, the night she'd learned the truth, Beau had said, almost accusingly, that Lola'd been covered in diamonds when he'd seen her on Cat Shoppe's stage. He must've thought very highly of her as a stripper if he'd believed that. They were actually rhinestones. She'd purchased the two-piece bikini in November during a Halloween clearance sale. It'd come in a plastic zip bag. At the register, she'd grabbed a pair of cat ears to top off the outfit. Every other girl at Cat Shoppe had had a thing, and she'd needed a thing. There'd already been a couple of feline-themed strippers, but none of them had sparkled like her.

But that was then, and this was now. Now, Lola had Beau—the kind of man who appreciated extravagance. The kind who expected his stripper to wear diamonds when he put her up on his pedestal.

"I'll take it," Lola said, "as well as black underwear and thigh-high stockings."

The saleswoman nodded. "Shoes?"

"I have them. Four-inch Louboutins."

"You must be looking to deliver quite a blow."

"Something like that." Lola opened her purse and pulled out Beau's weighty credit card. Before she handed it over, she paused as she was hit with an idea. "By any chance, do you carry cat ears here?"

"I'm sorry?" The woman's hand twitched, as if resisting reaching for the credit card. "I'm not sure what you mean."

Lola held her hands on both sides of her head and pointed upward. She wiggled her fingers. "You know, like the ones you wear on Halloween?"

"Oh. No. Of course we don't."

"Hmm." Lola tapped the card against her bottom lip, thinking. "That could really pose a problem for my outfit."

"I'll take care of it." The saleswoman watched the card, her eyes fixed on the rhythmic back and forth. She held her hand out. "I'll find some and have them delivered wherever you like along with your purchase."

Lola smiled and handed over the credit card. "That would be fantastic. They don't need to be anything fancy. I'll take the lingerie with me, but I'd like those sent somewhere else."

"That won't be a problem, Miss…" She checked the card. "Olivier."

Lola paid for everything and returned to the Range Rover, which she'd parked at a meter. She slipped into the front seat and rested her hands on the steering wheel, but she didn't turn the engine on. She glanced at herself in the rearview mirror. What a funny thing money was—it bought not only things, but people's time. Lola had discovered how true that was since she'd been by Beau's side. Just now, in the store, she'd used her newfound wealth as leverage to get what she wanted. Was it too much time around Beau that had Lola acting like someone she didn't recognize? Or was that just how money worked, no matter who you were? It was addicting to have it that easy, and part of her understood, for the first time, how complicated Beau's relationship with his fortune must be.

Lola shook her head quickly. She couldn't think too hard about Beau this late in the game. It was as simple as this—Beau wasn't the man she'd thought he was, and for that he deserved whatever was coming to him. Three weeks had seemed like a lifetime to fake all the things she had—forgiveness, affection, submission. Now that it was ending, she worried she wasn't prepared. Beau was used to getting his way, which meant a number of things could go wrong. Lola needed to keep her head in the game and a sway in her hips. It was a delicate operation, pulling the string that unraveled him without yanking it. He'd been salivating over Lola for long enough now that he was right where she needed him. That was what she had to distract him with—his own crippling need. It was the art of misdirection, and the key to pulling off her magic trick.

◆ ◆ ◆

Cat Shoppe's music thumped so loudly, Lola felt it in her bones before she even reached the entrance. The bouncer took one look at her plum-colored vinyl miniskirt and opened the red velvet rope for her. Even in the middle of the day, several men and a couple women sat around the stages, drinks and dollar bills in their hands. The place stunk, as if the furniture was soaked nightly in vats of beer, and the men bathed in cheap cologne.

She'd changed in the Range Rover, sinking down in the backseat to swap her Alexander McQueen dress for a vintage concert tee. She'd smeared her perfectly-applied lipstick onto a tissue before caking on glitter eye shadow.

At the bar, she ordered a shot of tequila as reinforcement from a girl in a platinum-blonde wig. At least, Lola thought it was a wig, the way it poofed around her chipmunk cheeks and met under her chin like a heart. This time, the tequila didn't make Lola wince the way it had in Beau's car up on Mulholland Drive. It was courage. She'd never grimace after a shot again if she could help it.

The bartender took the glass back. "Another?"

"No, thanks." Lola dug a twenty out of her pocket and put it on the bar. "I'm here to see Kincaid."

"You looking for a job?"

"Not really."

"Good, because there's not enough to go around as it is. As you can see, I've got to work the bar just to make some extra cash." She took Lola's bill off the bar and went to the register.

"Keep the change," Lola said.

She turned back. "Really? It was three dollars."

Lola waved a hand. "It's fine."

"Cool." She stuffed the money in her white bikini top, not even cashing out the shot. She fixed the string of her bottoms, then looked up and caught Lola watching her. "Marilyn," she said, pointing at the drawn-in birthmark on her upper lip. "Monroe?"

"Oh." Lola nodded.

"Also known as Susan, but that's not really my gig."

"Nice to meet you."

Marilyn-Susan refilled Lola's glass with tequila and set it in front of her. "On the house. You dance?"

Lola picked up the shot. "Not anymore. I worked here a while back, though."

The girl's breasts bounced when she clapped her hands together. "Really? So you know Glinda the Good Bitch?"

Lola smiled hearing her old friend's name. Glinda'd been stripping as long as she'd had something to show. She'd taken Lola under her wing just like she always did with the new girls, kind of like a mentor. They'd grown apart when Johnny'd come along, though. He'd forbidden her from going on a girls' trip to Vegas, and after that, she'd begun to lose touch with the group. "I used to, yeah. Best dancer this side of Hollywood."

"Not lately. Been hitting the blow too hard. She's in a bad state."

Lola glanced down at the bar. The news didn't surprise her, considering how easy it was to get sucked into that life. She almost had. A lot of girls, some she knew, many she didn't, had gone too far down the path Johnny had pulled Lola back from. She was indebted to him in a way she could never repay, and no matter their history, she'd never forget that.

"I'll go grab Kincaid," Marilyn said, walking away.

While Lola waited, she looked over her shoulder at the girl writhing on stage. Her hard nipples grazed the floor as she danced for the dollar bills fanned around her.

"She's got nothing on you," said a man behind her.

Lola turned to see Cat Shoppe's owner. "Kincaid."

"Lola." He put his hand on the back of her stool and kissed her cheek. "Or do you go by Melody now?"

"Still Lola."

Marilyn was back behind the bar. "Was Melody your stage name?"

"No. It's my full name, but I don't use it."

"Melody," Marilyn repeated. "Like a song. That's sweet."

Sometimes, she thought her given name was the only thing her mom liked about her since she'd picked it out. Lola had once cried as a kid about not having a middle name, though, so her dad had told her it could be Lola, short for Melody. The nickname'd stuck, and Lola had a theory Dina had taken it personally.

Back in the day, Lola was the only one at the club who'd danced under her real name, the rest of the girls making up something sugary and anonymous.

Lola turned to face Kincaid completely as he pulled up a seat next to her. "So, how are you, Kincaid?"

"It's been a while."

"Not as long as you think," she said.

"Aha. So that *was* you I saw on the security camera a few weeks ago."

Lola hadn't seen Kincaid when she'd come to Cat Shoppe with Beau, but she remembered his diligence when it came to security. He almost always had someone on the cameras, making sure his customers stayed in line. "Yep. Kind of an unexpected trip down memory lane."

"With someone who's got money to burn." Kincaid gave her a once over. "That guy you were with? You wouldn't believe what he paid for a room, two of our girls and some privacy."

"Actually, I would believe it." When she swallowed, she tasted tequila. Tequila and Beau, that first night she'd put her lips on him. "I hope you didn't watch the whole show."

He smiled cautiously. "Seen enough couples come through here to know when to look away. What I did see, though, was good. Can't fake that kind of love for the dance."

"Actually, that's why I'm here." Lola cleared her throat. The backs of her thighs had begun to sweat, turning the stool's leather tacky against her skin. She needed Kincaid tonight, or her entire plan could go to shit. "The man I came with last time loved the show so much, I want to give him another."

Kincaid shrugged. "Not a problem. Same girls, or—?"

"Just me," Lola said. "He has a kind of fascination with watching me dance."

"Right. Angel and Golden said it was the easiest money they ever made. The guy barely looked at them the whole time they were in VIP."

Lola nodded and tucked her hair behind her ear. She'd definitely had his attention that night. "I want him to have a real, true-life, gritty experience, though. As if I worked here, and he wandered in off the street."

"You want a room for a few hours, you got it. I have to charge you, but—"

"Money isn't the issue. What I'm asking for is—I want to be…one of your girls again. Just for tonight."

Kincaid narrowed his eyes, searching her face. "I'm not sure what you're getting at. Can't be good, though. You look like the cat that swallowed the canary."

"It's good," Lola said, reassuring, nodding. "There's a lot of money in it for you if you play along."

Kincaid made an inviting gesture with his hand. "I'm listening."

"This is how it'll go. Tonight, I work for you. I belong to you—no one else. I want him to have the full experience."

"You said that already."

She leaned forward, conspiring with him, looking into his eyes. "I want your protection."

"My protection?" He absentmindedly picked at some peeling plastic on the countertop. "Sounds serious. What about your bartender a few blocks down? As I recall, you two were pretty tight."

"We're not together anymore."

"That so? Completely done? Because he was the reason you left all this behind."

Lola ran her tongue along her upper teeth. "Yeah, well. Things change."

"What things?"

"You ask a lot of questions." She flipped her hair over her shoulder. "Do we have a deal?"

"You know how I am about my girls and my business. It's all I got. I don't need any jealous boyfriends coming through that door."

"He won't. Trust me—Johnny and I are through. So, can you do this for me? I told you, there's good money in it for you."

"I'll do anything for you, Lola, soon's I understand what you're asking me."

Lola shifted in her seat. Some people were not as easily bought as others, and that would've given her some comfort if she didn't need this last piece of the puzzle. "Customers don't come here expecting to take one of us home," she said. "It's like a fantasy, right? They watch us. They let us tease them. I could sit Beau in a kitchen chair and dance in his lap, but it wouldn't be the same. There, I'm his girlfriend who he gets to fuck after. But here? It's a game, and I'm a prize he can't have."

Kincaid nodded. He was no idiot—he understood her. He'd made a living off keeping women just outside of men's reach. "What do you need me to do?"

Lola opened her purse. "I'll pay you now. Cash. I'll explain the rules to Beau over dinner. But as soon as we walk in the door, he's a customer, and I'm an employee. I'll take him to the VIP room. Just watch him, and make sure he behaves."

"You know we got the big rules here. For the employees, bottoms stay on, no sexual activity. For customers, it's no touching unless the dancer initiates it, and even then, it's all over the clothing."

"Exactly. I'm not agreeing to allow any of that."

"All right. So what if he doesn't behave?"

"Same as if any customer were to touch one of your girls." Lola handed over enough cash to rent the VIP room for an entire night, though she didn't think she'd need even an hour. "You don't let him get away with it."

Chapter Ten

Beau stared at the buildings just outside his office window, a whiskey in his hand. All day, he'd been wondering about tonight, what this secret was Lola had planned, how long she'd make him wait for the main course. He was eager to get his last meeting over with so he could go home to her.

He was becoming someone he didn't recognize. Work had always been his constant, but the only thing that calmed him now was her—specifically, the security of having her in his arms where he could see and feel her. He'd thought paying for her had been the way to own her, but he'd been so off base, it almost made him laugh. Knowing she loved him enough to let him earn her trust again—that was how he owned her, how she owned him.

Except that today, just knowing that wasn't enough. He was restless, and he needed more. He'd always been able to read Lola, but that morning in the foyer, it was as if he'd been looking into someone else's eyes. Since their reunion, she hadn't kissed him with that much enthusiasm. Something was off.

Beau sipped his drink. She was nervous about tonight. As she should be. Beau wiped a bead of sweat from his forehead. He hadn't had to wait this long for something he wanted in a decade. Almost three impossible weeks of watching Lola, touching her, kissing her, sleeping next to her—all of it with restraint. He was ravenous, and only she would satisfy him. The thought of another woman did nothing for him, not that it really ever had. Until Lola, he hadn't known what it'd meant to truly bury himself inside someone and be willing trade the world just to have her come. Giving her that kind of pleasure was as addicting as having any part of her around his cock.

It was a sweet kind of torture, coming home from work and watching her get ready for his events. That was why he took her so many places. He loved to sit on their bed as she picked out a dress, hiding in the closet while she changed.

She would come over to the bed and turn her head over her shoulder. "Zip me?"

He would stand and obey. Fabric would swallow the lacey edges of her undergarments as he zipped her dress, the only morsels she'd throw him. He wasn't even sure she knew how those small slices tempted him. He'd let his knuckle brush along her spine, thinking, *"Soon, I will get to touch all of you again. Soon."*

Lola wore perfume on those nights, and it would stick to his suits, linger in her hair. Before it could fade completely, there'd be some other occasion to dress up for. He wondered if she'd always applied her makeup so carefully, coating mascara on her lashes with long strokes and gliding eyeliner on with the kind of concentration she didn't even give him. It bothered him that he couldn't remember the exact details of the night he'd met her at Hey Joe, like whether or not she'd been wearing that much makeup. He would never forget how blue her eyes were or the noisy leather of her pants, but that wasn't enough. He wanted to remember everything.

He'd been skeptical that anything could give him as much satisfaction as his work, but Lola did, even without the sex. That was why he devoted his days to making sure she'd never want for anything—to be able to give her anything upon request. He'd worked hard before, but now, he *labored* for her. Late nights would always belong to them, though. After events and long hours at the office, that was when he'd get as close to her as she'd let him, and then he'd always try for a little closer.

Beau walked through the quiet house to the bedroom, his fingers pulling impatiently at his bowtie. Lola had been living there four days, and everything had changed. Just having her on his arm at tonight's gala had turned a chore into a chance to show her off to anyone who'd look. And even though it'd been a form of torture to stand by her all night and keep his hands to himself, it'd been worth it to see her at her most exquisite. The only other times he'd been this high were his first two nights with her, undressing her, touching her skin as slowly and as quickly as he could. He wasn't ready to let that feeling go.

He entered his bedroom. Through a sliver of doorway, Lola moved around the bathroom in her robe, removing makeup from her face, jewelry from her body. He pushed open the door and went to where she stood at the sink. He'd promised to behave, but after tonight, he wasn't sure he could. God knew he didn't want to. He slipped his arms around her waist and buried his face in the sweet scent of her hair. "You already changed?" he whispered. "I wanted to watch."

Since she'd come back a few days earlier, he'd been careful about touching her. When he did, she'd tense up. This time, though, she remained calm. Maybe it was the wine from the gala or maybe, he hoped, she was feeling the same thing he was tonight.

"I never let you watch," she said.

"That doesn't mean I don't."

There it was—the delicate but noticeable stiffening of her body. But at the same time, her breathing sped. He'd missed that—the way she would fight her arousal with him.

"You watched me?" she asked huskily.

"Mmm." He moved her hair aside and kissed a spot under her ear. To watch her undress would most certainly mean losing control. She'd been fluid in the long gown she'd worn tonight, and he wanted to see what was underneath. Desperately. To reach his hand into the tight neckline and take one of her perfect tits. "No," he said. "But it's been very tempting."

Beau started at a knock on his office door. He rubbed the corners of his eyes, trying to dissipate the haze brought on by thoughts of fucking Lola. Just a few more hours until he'd get back there again, and he could barely see straight from anticipation.

"What is it?" he called out.

"Your four o'clock is here."

He was hard. Fuck. Still staring out the window at downtown Los Angeles, he wondered who out there had worked for him at some point or another. That was a game he played to calm himself sometimes—how many people depended on him to stay afloat?

God, he was a sick bastard.

"Five minutes," he told his assistant, swigging the last of his drink. He willed his cock to relax as he tried to think of anything but Lola's soft, naked body, warm everywhere from weeks of wanting him.

Waiting for him.

He didn't deserve her, but that made him even more grateful. He planned to spend all his nights reversing the pain he'd caused her. And to think—he'd almost lost her.

No, Beau didn't recognize the person he'd become, but he didn't mind. He was forever changed that night he'd thought he'd lost her for good, only to walk into the lounge of the Four Seasons hotel and find her.

Waiting for him.

Chapter Eleven

Three weeks earlier

At exactly 9:51 P.M. on the same day she'd fled Beau's presidential suite, Lola slipped into a high-backed seat at the hotel's lounge. She'd passed out on the floor of her eleventh-floor room for a few hours, but after a cold shower, she'd slipped back into her white dress. She was reborn—and ready to enter the arena.

Revenge went against her nature, but Lola's motive ran as deep as Beau's betrayal had cut. This wasn't eye for eye or tooth for tooth—it was the most valuable thing you could give another person. Hope for a future, raw vulnerability. This was heart for heart.

"Evening." The bartender slid a napkin in front of her. "What're you having?"

Lola's back was unnaturally straight, her body tense. Tonight, she was both predator and prey, target and huntsman. It was an entirely normal inquiry from a bartender—what drink did she want—but she'd come to learn that friendly strangers were strangers nonetheless, and strangers could be dangerous. She repositioned herself in the chair, trying to get more comfortable. "What do you recommend?"

He grabbed a menu from the bar and held it open in front of her. He tapped it with his finger. "I'm new here, but I'm told the Colony Cocktail is our most popular drink."

Lola's mouth soured. The last man who'd picked her drink had also chosen that one, and it hadn't exactly turned out well. "I'll have anything but that."

He laughed, clapped the menu closed and tossed it aside. "How about I make you my off-menu specialty?"

She tried to smile, but it felt more like a grimace. The bartender was a poor distraction. Beau could be back any minute, she had no idea. "Sounds great. I also need a Macallan, neat."

"You got it." He picked out a couple liquor bottles and moved down the bar.

Lola released a breath. She was tempted to turn and check the entrance, but she kept her eyes forward and her back to the door. To put him at ease, he had to believe he was in charge, that he could sneak up on her.

The bartender set down both drinks, and Lola moved the Scotch to the side. She unsnapped her clutch.

"It's on the house."

Lola looked up from her lap. She'd worked in a bar a long time, and drinks never came free. "But the Macallan. It's expensive."

He shrugged. "It's my second night here, and my manager left me alone. Why not?"

Lola closed her purse. "You won't get in trouble, will you?"

"Maybe, but it'd be worth it. If I could get a smile."

There it was, the price of her drink. A little bit of herself. And surely, he expected her to be flattered by his manipulation. It occurred to Lola, she'd agreed to a game of darts with Beau knowing little more about him than she did about this bartender. It'd led to a more dangerous game.

He stood there, waiting, not reading her skepticism.

She smiled. At least she knew better now. "Thank you. What is it?"

"Blood orange juice and gin." He glanced between her eyes and the red drink. "Strawberries on top. It's called an *Amore Vietato.*"

"Amore." Lola picked up the martini glass and took a sip. "That's Italian for love, isn't it?"

"Yes."

"What's vietato mean?"

"Forbidden."

She shifted her eyes to meet his. A love that shouldn't exist, that survived despite the odds. Or because of them?

"Excuse me," he said when another customer sat a few seats down.

Lola checked her watch and glanced around. It was after ten o'clock. The bar was right off the lobby, but the hushed conversations and low lights made it feel secluded. It was made for seduction, but that was only half the reason she'd chosen it. She wanted to remind Beau of the hour they'd spent there on their second night, their drinks barely touched, her mouth closer to his than necessary.

Like any woman worth her salt, Lola could fake intimacy, but men weren't wired that way. Beau's adoration had been in his touch, his eyes, his whispered words. Even if it was only an ember, something burned in him for her.

Lola sipped her Amore Vietato and took comfort in the fact that even roaring, rampant fires had started as embers.

Minutes passed. When Lola's posture began to slouch, she corrected it.

The bartender returned and leaned his hip against the counter. "So, what is it? Blind date?"

Lola shook her head. "Just a friendly drink with a…friend."

"Right." He raised an eyebrow. "That dress is about as opposite of friendly as it gets."

Lola cocked her head. "You think?"

He dropped his gaze for the briefest moment. "If he's male, your friend might get the wrong idea."

"And I guess that would be my fault."

"Of course. You know what you're doing. Nothing is ever as it seems with you ladies."

Lola stuck her elbows on the counter like she and the bartender were old friends. "That's a lot to put on an article of clothing."

"My ex wore white when she'd done something especially devilish. It was a subconscious way of seeming innocent so I'd take pity on her."

She squinted at him. There was no ring on his hand. Not even a tan line where a ring would be. That didn't mean anything, though. A ring could change a person's entire identity, and it could also be slipped on and off. Like her, he was black-haired and blue-eyed, but his face was round and inviting. Her face was not round, it was heart-shaped, and she doubted it was particularly inviting tonight. That would have to change once Beau got there.

She lifted one shoulder. "What if a dress is just a dress?"

The saleswomen of Rodeo Drive had shown Lola many outfits earlier that day. Red was aggressive. Black was too *her*—she didn't want to be herself tonight. She only wanted to play herself. White'd been the least threatening. Perhaps the bartender had something there.

"It's just a theory," he said, another shrug. "I never asked her. Then she'd know I was onto her."

Lola was leaning a little farther over the bar now, envisioning what Beau would see if he'd walk in right then. "Sounds like you two had some trust issues."

"Show me a relationship without trust issues, and I'll show you bullshit." He laughed, genuinely amused, then scanned her face. "I'm Sean, by the way."

She shook his outstretched hand. "Lola."

"Beautiful name for a beautiful woman."

Lola rolled her eyes. He wouldn't have said that if she'd been herself, normal clothing, just a girl having a beer. This dress, this hotel in this part of town, it was like a parallel universe. "Surely you can do better than that."

He shook his head, shamefaced but grinning. "You're right. How about—an angelic name for an angelic dress. As for the woman in it…"

"Not angelic?" she suggested, crooking the corner of her mouth.

"That's to be determined." He winked, then looked over her shoulder, his expression souring like he'd just eaten something questionable.

Lola didn't have to ask what'd caused that look. Something ghosted against her ear, causing the hair on the back of her neck to stand on end.

The familiar voice was deep, warm and unequivocally male, but Lola sensed the edge in his words. "What are you doing here?"

She turned to face him, the man she loved and loathed, her expression soft and her hands balled into quiet fists—fragile as a vase hiding igneous rock.

Chapter Twelve

Beau loved Lola's hair—to feel it between his fingers, to pull it in a fist as he took her from behind. She responded to that as much as he did, arching and moaning toward the ceiling. Even with her back to him in the hotel lounge, there was no mistaking her shiny hair, obsidian-black against her white dress.

Lola turned her head over her shoulder, hesitating a moment before she looked up at him. After the way they'd parted in the early hours that morning, he would've expected anger. Their time together had been short, but he'd learned to read her mood through her eyes—she was calm.

"I'm sorry." She sighed as if she'd been holding her breath a long time. "To just show up this way. I didn't know where else to go."

Beau stood up straighter. He was more than a part of her world—he was all of it. She had nowhere to go—because of him. Yet she'd returned. Why? She wasn't the type to come slinking back.

He reluctantly shifted his gaze from Lola to the bartender, who needed to be dealt with before either of them said another word. Beau'd walked in on an unpleasant scene—Lola, in an uncharacteristically sexy dress, getting winked at by a bartender. Hadn't Beau taught her about the dangers of unfamiliar men? As the day had passed, he'd been less convinced she'd broken things off with Johnny. *Johnny*, who deserved his balls in a vise, might still have Lola, and that brought Beau's blood to a boil. Now he had to worry about the entire male species?

"You must be new here," Beau said.

The man crossed his arms. "And you are?"

"A man with a very helpful tip." Beau picked up the amber drink next to Lola and studied it, his upper lip curling. "The staff is here to serve, not to enjoy my things."

Lola glanced up at Beau.

"I don't understand," the bartender said.

"The valet doesn't take my car out for a joyride. The housekeeper doesn't wear my Rolex while she cleans." Beau put his other hand on the back of Lola's chair. "You look at her like that one more time, I'll have you fired."

The man's jaw dropped into a disbelieving, open-mouth smile. "Dude, I was keeping her company. Bugs me to see such a beautiful woman waiting on anyone."

He unfolded his arms and set his palms on the edge of the bar, leveling a glare at Beau. "Especially someone who just referred to her as one of his possessions."

"Don't, Sean," Lola said in warning. "It's not your problem."

For Lola's sake, Beau refrained from explaining that up until recently, she had been his possession. The way she'd referred to Beau as a problem, though, he was tempted. Instead, he slid his glass across the bar. "This isn't Macallan."

"It'll have to do." Sean pushed the glass back. "We're fresh out."

"We can go somewhere else." Lola tried to stand, but Beau put a heavy hand on her shoulder, keeping her in her seat.

"If you'd like to keep your job past the end of this conversation," Beau said, ignoring her, "you should check again."

"My job?" Sean raised his eyebrows. "I'm sorry—I wasn't aware I had a new boss."

"I'm worse than your boss—I'm a guest here. An important one. Make my drink, and put both mine and hers on my tab."

Lola shifted in her seat. "Mine was on the house."

"No, it's not." Beau didn't take his eyes off the guy, who wouldn't have felt like a threat any other time, but Lola being suddenly there was throwing him off. "Charge it to my room. Beau Olivier."

Sean blinked once and pushed off the bar, taking a step away. "You're Mr. Olivier?"

"That's right."

"Of course. I'm so sorry." Sean picked up Beau's drink and set it down again. "I didn't realize—I just started here. I thought you'd be...different. Like an old guy."

"How about that drink?" Beau was eager to get back to Lola. From the corner of his eye, he could see her staring up at him, her eyes wide, like he was God. It was making his pants tight.

"Yes, sir," Sean said, turning in almost a complete circle as he mumbled to himself, "Beau Olivier, Macallan, neat. I knew that."

Not until the bartender was out of earshot did Beau look back at Lola. "When I talk to the manager, that poor kid'll be fired. Because of you. Doesn't that make you feel bad?" Beau slid his hand down her shoulder, tracing a finger along the low-cut neckline of her dress. Less than five minutes, and he had the overwhelming need to touch her again. "Or does that kind of power over another person turn you on?"

Lola closed her hand around his, stopping it in its tracks. "I didn't come here to screw you."

"What makes you think I want to?"

She glanced down at his pants and licked her lips, forcing Beau's eyes directly to her now-glistening pink mouth. He'd done unspeakable things to that mouth, and to her round tits, her flat, quivering tummy. And the first time he'd touched the petal-soft skin of her inner thighs, parted them like the sea, it'd been with ten years' worth of anticipation.

"My mistake," she said smoothly, drawing his attention back up. She glanced over at Sean, who was pouring Beau's drink.

Beau took her chin and turned her face to his. "Don't look away from me."

She just blinked at him. "I'm not."

"You're alone?"

She swallowed.

"Is it over?"

"Do you want it to be?"

Beau didn't answer right away. He was having trouble reading her for the first time. Without knowing why she was there or what exactly she wanted, he wasn't about to admit anything she could use against him. "It makes no difference to me."

Her expression stayed clean, but her cheek twitched. "You were right about him."

Beau's hand tightened a little around her jaw. He was on edge, and he didn't want to hear about Johnny, but that statement wasn't something he could ignore. "What was I right about?"

"A lot of things." Her voice had softened— because of his hand? Or because she was hurting? "He was with Amanda last night while I was here."

His mouth was closed, but he ground his teeth hard. It didn't surprise him. Beau had seen Johnny for the coward he was the night he'd met him in Hey Joe. For one, Johnny hadn't beaten Beau to a pulp for propositioning Lola. He was weak, selfish. Beau considered himself above physical altercations, but right then, he wished he'd taken a swing at Johnny when he'd had the chance.

Beau loosened his grip a little. "I warned you that would happen."

"It's not the reason we broke up," she said, her voice hedging but her intent clear, like she wanted him to know that. "By the time I found out, we were already done. There's so much more to it than that."

Beau didn't need to hear the reasons. He nodded. "I know."

"You asked why I'm here—that's why. My mom and I don't speak. I don't really have anyone else. If I go back to my apartment—"

"You're not going back there."

She shied away as much as she could while in his grip, which wasn't much. "Then where am I going?"

Beau didn't have an answer for that. He wasn't sure why he'd even said it. The idea that he wasn't ready to let Lola go had been growing on him all day, but now it was a fact. He wasn't finished with her, and she was there, but that didn't mean he understood why he was happy about it. "You could go to the eleventh floor."

Her lips parted, a small gasp. "You knew I was staying here?"

He almost laughed at her shock. Had she learned nothing about him and what he was capable of the past few weeks? "I saw you in the lobby earlier."

Her eyebrows gathered. "When I checked in? Have you been—following me or something?"

"You walked right by me." Beau ran the pad of his thumb under her chin and tsked. "Didn't even notice. You really should be more careful, ma chatte."

"How do you know my room number?"

Beau didn't know which room she was in, but he could find out before she'd even finished her drink—the one turning her mouth an affected shade of red. "It's my business to know these things."

She scoffed. "What I do is none of your business. You made sure of that."

Beau cocked his head. Finally, a reaction—the fire that excited him as much now as it had the first night they'd spent together. "You should know by now—if I want to, I make it my business." She tried to look away, but Beau wasn't about to let that fire go out now that he'd sparked it. "What're you really here for?" he asked. "An apology?"

She shook her head. "Words could never make it right, what you did."

It didn't matter. Beau's plan had never had a second part. Once he'd dropped the axe on their connection, it was supposed to have severed any hope of redemption, of reconciliation. Like any deal worth making, he'd been ruthless, anticipating Lola's every move, manipulating her to his own end. He'd proven he could buy things that couldn't be bought. He was a master at something that couldn't be mastered.

So why did he feel as if he'd lost something? After he'd gone through so much to own her for those two nights, she didn't belong to him now. When they parted ways tonight, she wouldn't be where he could see her. She wouldn't come when he called.

Beau released her face. "What could?"

Lola raised her chin, her eyes narrowing almost imperceptibly. "You're asking me how to make this right?"

She was as proud as he was, yet she'd come back. Her feelings for him were even stronger than he'd thought. Was love that overpowering, that healing? Was Lola finding the strength to move past the pain, to accept Beau's flaws—in the name of love? It was as if some softer, calmer version of her sat in front of him instead of the real thing. The problem was, Beau had fallen for the real thing—the girl who'd stopped him in his tracks when she'd put a dent in a car with her Converse.

"I'm asking if it can even be made right."

Lola glanced down at her hands, laced in her lap. Her knuckles were white from pressing her palms together. With a deep breath, she relaxed her fingers and looked up at him. Not a single muscle on her face moved until finally, she blinked. "Yes. If you want that."

"I'm missing something here," Beau said. "You were irate this morning. You should be broken."

"*Should* be?" Lola asked, raising an eyebrow. "If I'm not, does that mean you failed?"

He opened his mouth. Did it? Did Beau have his power back if he hadn't actually hurt her as much as he'd thought? There was no outcome to this where they both won. "No, I didn't fail. You're hurt, angry, confused. You want to know why I did this."

"Yes, all of that's true. That doesn't mean I don't still l—," she hesitated but continued to look him in the eye, "care about you."

Beau was suddenly warm in his suit. It'd been so long since he'd slept, he could almost convince himself he'd misheard what she'd been about to say. He didn't doubt she loved him still—that didn't change overnight. But love was anger and hurt and demanding the truth. He didn't want this person, who was turning a blind eye. He wanted more, because when she loved him—*that* was power.

"Do you remember Hank Walken?" Beau asked.

Lola's jaw shifted left then right. "How do you know Hank Walken?"

"He works for me."

"He's slime."

"That's why I keep him around." Walken had done things for Beau he couldn't have done for himself. Reaching for a dream was nice, but those who got there had to grab it by the throat, kill or be killed. Sometimes, it wasn't pretty, what had to be done. "He'll do anything for a buck. Like make a fake offer on Hey Joe."

"It wasn't fake. He was going to turn it into a rooftop bar. A lounge with—with celebrities, and..." They stared at each other, Beau watching the realization hit. "That was never going to happen?"

"Not on my watch. Hey Joe is a dump. Wasn't worth my time." Beau brushed Lola's hair over her shoulder. "My time, my money—they were better spent on other things."

"Were they? You're such a savvy businessman? By my calculation, you lost big time on this deal. If you pit Walken against me and Johnny, then you knew Johnny and I would have to come back to you with a higher counteroffer for the first night. That would put you in a bidding war with yourself."

Beau nodded. It was, by far, the most careless he'd ever been with his money, and that hadn't been easy. But it'd almost been unavoidable, the seed of the idea planted early, maybe even on the sidewalk before they'd spoken.

"Walken put pressure on you to make a decision," Beau said. "Johnny could justify anything because he'd never survive without Hey Joe. I knew that. More importantly, though, you knew it."

"So instead of five hundred thousand, which was already more than what Hey Joe was worth, you drove the price up to a million."

"No, actually. My offer was always a million."

Her nostrils flared, but he could see she still didn't understand. "It was five hundred. Trust me, a girl doesn't forget the first time someone assigns her a dollar amount."

"It was always a million." Beau sniffed. He'd wanted to protect her in the hotel room that morning with Brigitte's text, but instead she'd wanted the truth. That's what he'd give her.

"I don't understand."

"I've dealt with many Johnnys in my life, and I knew he'd come back with a counteroffer. If I could get you to consider five hundred, there was no way you'd turn down twice that."

Lola jutted her chin out, the cogs turning in her mind as she pieced the puzzle together. "You lowballed us. I knew I was being manipulated, but this is something else."

"It's basic negotiation," Beau said. "Getting you into my bed was no different than any other business transaction. It should bring you some comfort to know it wasn't all personal."

"Comfort?" Lola snapped, jumping up from her stool. "You can't treat people that way—commodities to be traded and moved around however suits you." Her white cheeks were tinted pink, and the spark in her eyes had returned.

It reminded Beau of the first night when they'd argued, moments before he'd turned her around and fucked her against the hotel room window. Beau's blood also rushed a little quicker. "I treat people how they allow me to treat them," he said slowly. "You seem to forget I never forced you into a single thing."

"Exactly. You made me ask for these things, beg for them. Fuck you." She snatched her purse and turned away. "This isn't worth it."

Beau refrained from grabbing her arm like he wanted. They weren't finished until he said they were, and he wasn't ready to walk away yet. Especially after a comment he didn't understand. "What isn't worth it?"

Lola turned back and came right up under his chin. "After the first night, Johnny and I thought we had the bar, but we were in over our heads. What about that?"

"You agreed to buy something you couldn't afford. At the end of the day, that's why you took the second offer."

"But you knew all along that would happen. You made it so I'd have no choice but to accept your second offer." She smirked. "It's a shame you weren't confident enough in your abilities alone."

"Oh, I was," Beau said. "Nobody comes as hard as you did and doesn't crawl back for seconds. Or thirds…"

Lola raised her hand to slap him, but he caught her wrist before she could. "You're heartless," she spat, breathing hard. Her hair fell over one eye as she struggled to get her arm back. "There's nothing there, where your heart should be—just a big, fat dollar sign."

He loved the way she tried to take him on, every time she did it. Too much. He was getting hard, and he had a weakness for her—the combination of the two was like poison to his control. "Keep pushing my buttons. See what it gets you."

"I couldn't be any worse off than I am right now." She jerked her entire body, and he released her so she stumbled backward.

"No?" he asked. "Let's go, then. What you need is a good, hard spanking for your behavior tonight and an even better orgasm to ease the sting."

She gaped, her mouth opening wider, presumably to tell him off, but nothing came. She snapped her jaw shut. "That's all it ever was to you."

He couldn't tell if it was a statement or a question.

The lines around her eyes faded as she unwrinkled her nose. Her tone evened out. "Sex. Revenge. Fuck me, because I fucked you first."

He'd seen this look on her face before—losing her struggle to submit. It'd been the first time he'd brought her to his hotel and made her crawl to him. Lola had become so much more than a conquest that night— she'd fulfilled Beau's need for the impossible challenge he'd been looking for ever since he'd sold his first company. Beau was just as turned on now as he had been then.

"I have one last question," Lola said. "After that, if you want me to leave, I will."

Beau raised his eyebrows. If *he* wanted *her* to leave? She'd been in the middle of storming off, but she hadn't yet. And the longer she stayed, the less he wanted her to leave. More and more, he needed to take her upstairs and have the night they were never supposed to have.

"Was any of it real?" she asked.

Beau stared at her, almost angered by the question. He had told her *repeatedly* that it was real, both while it was happening and after the fact. How many times could he say it? Despite manipulating her, he'd never once lied to get her there. Lying would've been cheating to win, and Beau never cheated. He played ugly, but he played fair.

"Everything was real, every detail I shared with you. I never lied about my past or my family. Not about my feelings. If you hadn't read that text this morning, you would've gone home, broken up with Johnny, and I would've been here waiting for you when you got back."

Beau was breathing hard, but the admission came easily. His time with Lola had been so limited, he'd had to learn how to open up fast. Without that, he never would've had a shot at getting her to love him. Now, his honesty felt natural.

She searched his eyes. "The stars?" she asked quietly. "Why did you drive me up Mulholland Drive? Where did that fit into your plan?"

Beau's shoulders tensed. As they'd climbed the Santa Monica Mountains in his convertible, he'd glanced over at Lola. Her head had been tilted back to see the stars better, her hands cupped over her hair, loose strands flying around her face. She'd looked back at him right before he'd returned his eyes to the road.

Having her look at him that way—it'd been part of the plan. But the way it'd made him feel hadn't. Could he have possibly stopped that feeling, though? Earlier that night, he'd been inside her where nobody else had been. Her body had melted like butter underneath him, the last of her walls coming down. She'd trusted him, and she was his. He'd known it then. They'd always had an expiration date, but sudden and deep panic had hit him in the chest. He couldn't discard her, and he couldn't keep her.

"Mulholland was a moment of weakness on my part," Beau said carefully. "I thought it would make you happy."

"You didn't answer my question. Was it planned?" Her eyes dropped to his chest, and she closed them. "And the gas station?"

"What do you mean, the gas station?"

Lola was quiet as the question hung between them. Her insinuation became clear, and Beau would've laughed at the absurdity of it if it didn't feel like such a punch in the gut. "You're asking if I *planned* that?"

She opened her eyes. "You could've."

Beau rubbed his forehead hard. "You think I hired a man to rob us at gunpoint," he said evenly. The memory alone made his heart pound as if he were standing there again, completely helpless.

"I—"

"Hired him to scare the shit out of you. To put his hands on you."

"You've done worse."

She angled away from him a little, but he grabbed her shoulders, brought her close to look her straight in the eye. "I have never done worse than that. If you'd've let me, I would've gone after him. I would've hunted that motherfucker down and killed him for putting you in that position."

"I don't understand you," she said suddenly, her voice cracking. She bit her lip when her chin wobbled. "How do you do it?"

He released her immediately, stunned. Just the threat of her crying struck him, reminded him of how she'd broken down in his lap after the mugging and told him she loved him. She rarely showed vulnerability, that'd been clear to him within moments of meeting her. How many times had she cried since that morning? On her way home from the hotel? When she'd found out about Johnny and Amanda?

"How do I do what?" he asked.

"Turn everything off. Teach me how. If you can't love me, teach me how not to love you."

Beau's chest tightened. Lola was strong and stubborn. She wasn't this girl standing in front of him, submitting to her pain. Fighters, like Beau and Lola, turned sorrow into strength. He didn't know how to handle her as a girl whose heart he'd broken.

"I don't turn anything off." Beau's hands flexed in and out of balls. It took so little for her to turn him in a circle. His instincts about her were always changing, and that felt like losing control. "Do you think I liked watching you leave this morning? You never even gave me a chance to explain."

"Leaving was a mistake," she said bluntly but backed away.

Beau automatically stepped forward. He hadn't realized how much he'd wanted her to admit that.

"Or was coming here a mistake?" she continued. "I don't know, Beau. Should I not have come? Do you want me to leave? Tell me what to do."

Beau looked down at her. Her face was open, just like it'd been the night before when she'd trusted him with the biggest decision of her life. *I love you. I love him. Tell me what to do, Beau. I'll do it.*

Glenn Churchill had painted a picture of love for Beau—taking precious hours from his work to do absolutely nothing with Lola. Nothing but enjoy her company. Maybe they went to a coffee shop with friends, maybe they stayed in bed half the day. Not just a few times, but every weekend. Could he and Lola ever be that couple? The hurdle before them was massive.

"We aren't supposed to be together," Beau said.

Lola chewed her bottom lip. She stared at him, but she seemed lost in thought. "Okay. All right." After a brief hesitation, she turned around.

"Lola. Hang on." Beau rubbed the bridge of his nose. He closed his eyes, but he knew she was walking out. It was always going to end. It'd already gone on longer than it should've. Beau had never been good at ignoring his gut, though, and against all odds, it was telling him to go after her.

He crossed the room, strode through the lobby and caught up with her in the elevator bank, where she was waiting with her arms crossed.

"You didn't let me finish," Beau said.

She didn't even blink as she stared down the elevator doors.

"We're not supposed to be together. I don't see how it could ever work."

"Then let me go back to my room. I'll find a new hotel in the morning—or maybe I'll just go home. Either way, you won't see me again."

"I don't want that." Beau didn't like talking to her profile, but she avoided his eyes. "Come upstairs with me."

She exhaled a short laugh. "Upstairs? To your room? You must think I was born yesterday."

Beau raised his palms as if not to spook her. He might, if he didn't tread carefully. He regretted that he'd made a pass at her earlier. She suffered, because of him, and he was no longer sure he wanted that. "I don't think that, but it feels wrong for you to be here in my hotel and not with me."

She opened her mouth, but he continued before she could interrupt.

"I have a guest room. You can sleep there tonight, and after we've both gotten some rest, we can continue this talk."

The elevator arrived. Lola boarded it before the doors were even all the way open and hit a button.

He followed. "Lola."

She looked at him. "What?"

The doors closed. They were alone now—him, with Lola. He knew her, knew how to handle her, how to get her to respond. It was instinctual. "You're not going back to your room tonight."

"I see. Suddenly, you've decided you want me, and I'm just supposed to obey?"

"Neither of us knows what we want," he said. "But we both know you're not ready to walk away forever. Neither am I."

She readjusted her arms and tapped one gentle finger in sync with each *ding* of a passing floor.

"What do you need?" he asked. "Just to agree to come for tonight?"

She turned to face him without hesitating. "I need you to make me a promise. No matter what happens, no matter how good or bad it feels between us, no sex. I can't sleep with you right now. I'm too confused. I need to feel—safe...again."

"I understand."

"I don't just mean tonight. No, we don't know what's going to happen, but if it lasts a minute past tomorrow morning," she paused, "you can't touch me until I come to you and tell you I'm ready."

Beau sighed. He was exhausted—he'd have to be to agree to that. He would've said anything to get her up there so he could go to bed, though. Because he wouldn't be able to sleep without knowing she was in the next room.

It wouldn't be easy. Lola's power over him wouldn't go away just because he wished it would. That was becoming obvious.

"You have my word."

Lola looked at him a second longer and turned back toward the elevator doors. "Okay," she said. "I'll come."

It wasn't until they were walking to his room that he realized they'd never even stopped at the eleventh floor. When she'd gotten on the elevator before him, she'd pushed the button to go to the sixteenth.

Chapter Thirteen

Lying on her back, with her hands folded over her naked stomach, Lola stared up at the dark ceiling of Beau's guestroom. Beau'd kept his promise and shown her to the opposite side of the suite without so much as a handshake. From the dark circles under his eyes, she guessed he hadn't slept since well before she'd left him that morning.

She was tired too, but her thoughts were coming fast. Lola was far from the master Beau was. She hadn't had as much time to plot as he had, and she'd stumbled and faltered her way through their interaction tonight. He'd riled her. She'd almost walked away. It'd been risky, threatening to leave, but she was still here. And she wasn't ready to give in yet—she could learn this game.

She reviewed the evening with careful attention to detail—like his anger when she'd questioned his authenticity. It was most uncomfortable to turn the magnifying glass inward, though, to figure out what about Beau derailed her. She'd almost broken down learning the nuances of his layered plan.

She shouldn't have been surprised about Hank Walken's involvement—she might've figured it out if she'd given it enough thought. But the extent and depth of Beau's reach scared her. When Sean, the doting bartender, had turned from confident to cowering, Lola had realized how alone she was in this. Nobody could take Beau on, because there was nobody Beau's money couldn't buy.

Lola took a deep, meditative breath and closed her eyes, but not because she was going to sleep. She assumed somewhere out there, a star was shooting across the night sky. She made a wish—that Beau should suffer from his love the way she had. That she would be the first to bring him to his knees for what he'd done.

She had no choice but to return to a place she didn't want to. She had to be the Lola he'd fallen for in the middle of the night. The girl he'd touched as if she'd belonged to him rather than someone else. The girl who'd looked up at the stars and wondered how long ago her feelings for Johnny had begun to change. Who'd stepped in front of a gun for a man she hardly knew but one she knew she wasn't prepared to live without.

Beau had given her a picnic under the stars, but he'd also given her a pair of brand new Converse in her size when any old tennis shoes would've been fine. He paid attention when it counted and when it didn't. Lola's love for Beau was as fresh as the wound he'd left her with. That was good. She needed to feel the sting of both in order to pull this off.

She checked the clock by the bed. 2:17 A.M.

Lola folded back the comforter, swung her legs over the side of the mattress and stood. Beau had given her a robe, so she slipped into it. She easily knew her way to his room in the dark.

She stopped in his doorway. Her life had changed in that room. In that bed, she'd given him everything that'd meant anything to her. She had crawled across the floor to him, opened her legs to his mouth, bit the comforter as he'd broken down her last barrier. In that moment, Lola's love might've been hard to find, but her attraction to Beau was as loud as the beating of her heart. It was dangerous, and it'd require all of her strength to control it.

Lola tiptoed to the edge of his bed. His heavy, steady breaths told her he was sleeping peacefully. How could he not be when he'd gone so long without rest? She bent at the waist and peered at him in the dark. It would take nothing to hurt him. It would also be just as easy to fuck him. Was he naked? Did he dream of their two nights and what a third would be like?

His breathing stopped instantly. Before Lola could react, Beau's arm shot out and grabbed her robe by the belt. "What are you doing?"

She touched his hand at her waist, his skin radiating warmth. When he didn't object, she wrapped her fingers around his wrist. "I couldn't sleep."

"What do you want, a lullaby?" His tone was harsh, but his hand slipped inside the robe. Her breath stuttered as her body reacted to his touch in an alarming way—thawing as if it'd been frozen and waiting for heat. It disgusted her, the way Beau aroused her. He didn't deserve her, and he wouldn't have her—but he had to believe he could. She knew from experience, hope was one of the most painful things a person could lose.

Beau's palm flattened over her stomach and slid up around her waist. "Take this off," he said. "Come here."

She tightened the robe around herself but pulled back the covers and got in.

Beau sat up on an elbow and looked down at her. With his other hand, he touched the lapel of the robe. Lola's heart nearly stopped. He'd promised to respect her wishes, but did it matter? Wasn't it his way, to take what he wanted while making her think she wanted it too?

He moved his hand to her face, leaned in and kissed her. Every part of him was warm from sleep—his lips, the inside of his mouth, his breath. His thigh pressed against hers. She couldn't ignore the dull throb between her legs. No matter how much he'd hurt her, she'd always want this. But Beau had taken it away from her. This was his fault.

She didn't stop him right away. Men needed to touch and feel, to know she physically existed. It had to be done, and it had to be convincing, so she melted into the mattress, gripped his face and ran her fingertips down his scratchy cheeks. He opened his mouth wider, kissed her harder.

She pushed him back by his chest. They stared at each other, panting. "You promised," she said.

"*You* crawled into *my* bed."

"To be close to you."

"Let me get this straight." He placed his palm right below her throat, on the only skin the robe exposed. "You're asking me to sleep next to you and not touch you?"

If Beau moved his hand any lower, if he commanded her, Lola wasn't sure how she'd resist, but she had to. Her dignity was in shreds, but sleeping with him would destroy everything.

Lola rolled her lips together and glanced out toward the balcony, lit up from the moon. "I need time, Beau. You hurt me, and the worst part is, you did it on purpose. You can't expect me to—"

Beau sat up and switched on the bedside lamp.

Lola shielded her eyes. "What're you doing?"

"What do you think's going to happen when you come in here in the middle of the night? After everything we've been through in this exact spot?"

Lola reached over him and turned out the light. It was too harsh. Maybe she'd come to him too soon, but they needed to mend the bond they'd broken, and it had to be fast. Too fast for him to realize it was happening. "Do you want me to leave?"

He lay on his back again, looked up at the ceiling and sighed as if he carried the weight of the world on his chest. "No."

Lola put her hand on his bicep, softly stroking the hard muscle with her thumb. Touch was good—a weapon, even—as long as she could control it. "I'm not talking about your bed. Should I go?"

"I already told you. When I make a decision, it's done. I invited you here tonight. You aren't leaving." He rolled his head toward her, removed her hand from his bicep and pulled her down next to him. "Not this room. Not this spot."

Lola's body thrilled, but it was with a different kind of adrenaline. This feeling—this kind of *power* over someone—it wasn't like she'd never experienced it before, even with Beau. When her mouth was on his cock, or the moments right before she undressed, he'd get this look in his eyes like there was nothing he wouldn't do for her. This was something else, though. She was doing this to him with her words, using him against himself.

"Will you still feel that way tomorrow?" Lola asked. "What if—"

"I don't do 'what if,' Lola." Beau turned onto his side, put his arms around her and pulled her against his chest. He yawned in her ear. It was a moment before he spoke again, and his voice sounded far off. "Tomorrow is tomorrow. We'll deal with it then. If you're worried I'll wake up and…"

"And what?

"Change my mind…"

Lola waited, willing herself to stay perfectly still. If she tensed even one muscle, Beau would notice. That was the kind of attention she was dealing with. After a few seconds of silence, she realized he'd fallen asleep. "Beau?"

"Hmm?" He inhaled deeply and sighed. "What?"

"You said if I'm worried you'll wake up and change your mind…?"

He tightened his arms around her and whispered into her hair, "I won't."

He fell back asleep. She bit her lip to keep her relief inside and the smile from her face. It seemed to Lola that within only a few hours, she already had the bastard exactly where she wanted him.

Chapter Fourteen

Beau opened his eyes at 5:58 A.M. on the dot, just like every other morning. It didn't matter that he hadn't gotten enough sleep—routine was one of the secrets to his success. It kept him on track. It was the framework by which he measured his output.

This wasn't every other morning, though. Lola was in his arms. It didn't surprise him, but the memory of how she'd gotten there was foggy. Beau didn't like being woken up by anyone. It put him at a disadvantage. But if she hadn't, she wouldn't have been there in his bed that morning. And he liked her there.

He slid his arms out from under her and got up on an elbow. Her heart-shaped lips were parted for small, even breaths. He brushed a lock of hair from her cheek. Based on the previous morning, this was the last thing he would've expected to wake up to. Even knowing Lola loved him, he wouldn't have thought her pride would allow her to fight for him. She had a weakness for him the way he did for her.

Beau got out of the bed and pulled on his boxer briefs. Before leaving the room, he turned back and took his cell phone from the nightstand. God knew what kinds of incriminating things Brigitte might text him.

In the suite's kitchenette, he took two mugs from a cabinet. If Lola had slept as little as he did, she'd need caffeine when she woke. He rarely made his own coffee, but he didn't want to leave her alone to go get some. He got a pot started and checked on Lola to see if she was still asleep. She'd flipped over, her black hair strewn on the pillow like a sinister Sleeping Beauty.

He went to the foot of the bed, let his eyes travel the sheeted curves and bends of her body. He could take what he wanted from her. Waking her with a kiss would lead him between her legs in no time. He knew her body better than she did, how to touch it, read it, manipulate it. He traced the arch of her foot underneath the sheet, and she stirred.

His respect had to be earned. That was a tall order for the women he'd slept with. But he and Lola had been through enough that he felt he owed her at least that. It wasn't a stretch, not at all, to think he might love her. That was why he left the bed despite wanting to climb in next to her. He wouldn't keep his hands off her if he did.

He went out to the balcony and let the morning air cool his urges. The sky had shaded from black to cobalt, silhouetting the mountains against a blue as rich as

Lola's eyes. He closed the door to the room and called Brigitte.

"Beau?" she answered and cleared her throat. "What time is it? Is everything all right?"

"Sorry to wake you." He looked back at Lola through the windowed door. Her chest rose and fell rhythmically. This was what he'd missed those mornings she'd left at dawn. Anticipating the moment she'd wake up. Planning what they'd do with their day. "I'm coming home."

After a moment of silence, she spoke, the smile clear in her voice. "Well, that's news worth waking up for. I've missed having you around the house these past few weeks."

Beau kept watching Lola. He went out of his way to avoid fights with Brigitte, but this was one he needed to have. He wanted to do right by Lola from now on, and that wasn't stashing her away in a hotel room. "I'm not coming alone."

"Meaning?" She waited. "You're bringing someone over? Who?"

"We've been talking about getting you your own place for a while—"

"You've been talking about it," she said, sounding more awake now. "I haven't."

"I wouldn't ask you to go if I didn't think you'd like it. Being on your own." Over time, Brigitte had grown less independent and more reliant on Beau. He didn't mind taking care of her, but he planned on having Lola around a lot. And for her sake, he wanted his home back. "You have to trust me."

"Trust you?" she asked, her voice rising. "You're throwing me out on the street. How am I supposed to trust you?"

Beau closed his eyes and took a deep breath. He pinched the bridge of his nose. "Don't blow this out of proportion. I'll talk to my real estate agent today, and in the meantime, Warner and I will find you something temporary. You'll be more than comfortable."

"Pass me off to Warner like always. Did he know about this?"

"*I* didn't even know until just now. And I do not pass you off to Warner. Remember our conversation about wild exaggerations?"

"It's not an exaggeration. When was the last time you did anything for me that required more than making a phone call or writing a check? When I had that kidney infection last year, *Warner* took me to the hospital."

"And I paid your medical bills without flinching," Beau said evenly. "I'm your brother, not your employer."

"That's not the point. You wanted new furniture for the guestroom last month, so I got it. But you couldn't even come by the store to give me a second opinion on what I'd picked out. 'Just put it on the card, and have it delivered.' Whenever I need help or a ride or anything that doesn't absolutely require your presence, you send something else in your place. If it's not Warner, it's your credit card."

"Damn it, Brigitte, we've been through this before. I'm fucking busy. How do you expect me to take care of you if I'm not working my ass off?"

"Maybe I need to be taken care of in other ways," she snapped.

"I do as much for you as I'm capable of. I'm not your goddamn boyfriend. If you want someone to go shopping with you, find someone who has the time and inclination." Beau ended the call, gripping the phone. All people ever wanted from him was money, and he was fine with that. Why couldn't that be enough for Brigitte too? He didn't need to be constantly reminded of his shortcomings as a brother and a son. He gave his family what he could, and that was more than what ninety-nine percent of the world had. He held up his phone again, but this time he sent Brigitte a text.

Start packing. Will have arrangements for you by tomorrow.

He turned off his phone and went back inside.

Chapter Fifteen

Twenty-four hours after she'd stormed out of his hotel room vowing never to touch him again, Lola woke up in Beau's empty bed. She stood and tightened the belt of the robe she'd slept in. The balcony doors sat open, inviting a chill into the room. Lola stretched her arms toward the ceiling and refrained from patting herself on the back. She'd snuck into Beau's room in the middle of the night and had come out the other side in one piece. It was a small miracle she hadn't caved to his advances, but now she knew just what she was capable of.

"You're still here."

Lola looked over her shoulder. Beau stood on the other side of the bed with a towel around his waist and shaving cream all over his jaw.

"Why wouldn't I be?" she asked.

He pointed behind her. "Old habits."

Lola turned forward again. The rising sun sent pink and orange streaks across the sky—the moment Lola would be climbing out of Beau's limo back to Johnny. "I'm not leaving."

"I don't want you to," he called from the bathroom.

She followed his voice. Beau leaned over the sink. It was unfamiliar territory for them, the fresh scent of his shaving cream and the scrape of the blade over his stubble.

"I was worried you might change your mind this morning," she said.

He glanced briefly at her in the mirror's reflection. "I didn't."

"How do we do this?"

He dragged the razor up his cheek, mowing down each of the bristles Lola loved to feel against her face. Beau had enough money to buy a human, but apparently not an electric razor. That was him in a nutshell—rewards meant nothing if he hadn't worked for them.

He rinsed the blade under running water. "It's early. Why don't we eat before we start in on this?"

Lola's jaw tingled. The thought of eating breakfast food with him withered her insides. During their French toast meal the first night, her walls had begun to crumble—she'd even found herself *happy* despite how she'd gotten there. Reliving that would be more intimate than sleeping by his side. "I'm not hungry."

Beau splashed water on his jaw and, without warning, pulled the towel from around his waist. Lola swallowed her gasp before it escaped. She kept her eyes up, but it was nearly impossible not to peek.

He held her gaze as he patted his face dry, walked over and kissed her head. "Just coffee then," he said on his way out of the bathroom. "I already have some brewing."

When she was alone, she released her breath. She had to keep it together. This was the equivalent of entering his conference room to negotiate, and that'd been his first power play. Knowing him, there was more coming.

Lola returned to the bedroom, glancing around. Any trace she'd been there before then was gone. There was no lipstick on the comforter, and her beaded dress had been cleaned up. Beau'd probably thought removing her from his life was as easy as calling for maid service.

She went to the balcony and snuggled into her robe. It'd been out there, in the middle of their second night, that it'd hit her how much she'd already given Beau. It turned out, though, she hadn't given him anything. He'd taken it.

She rubbed her hands over her biceps. In that spot, Beau had held her so tightly, as if he'd thought she might disappear right before his eyes.

What if she had? What if one moment she'd been there, and the next she was gone, leaving him holding on to nothing but air?

"What're you thinking about?" Beau asked from behind her.

Lola looked back at him. He had two mugs in his hands and, thankfully, pajama pants on his body. "Why?"

"You're tense."

Lola forced her shoulders down from around her ears. Beau was a man who took great care when dealing with his adversaries, but she didn't have the resources or the practice he did. Honesty was one of her only weapons. "I was thinking about the last time we were out here. I was scared."

"Scared?" he repeated.

"Things were happening so fast. I was falling for you, and suddenly I realized that I didn't *have* to stop it. That I could fall, because—"

She stopped to let Beau's imagination fill in the blanks. At the same time, she pushed herself to relive those moments and tap into the pain that would fuel her.

He came up behind her. She sucked in a breath. Out of instinct, her muscles locked up. His touch could threaten her focus, and she could never forget that.

He set their coffee on the railing and wrapped her in his arms. "You're shivering."

"Am I?" She hadn't realized it.

"What were you going to say?" he prompted. "You could let yourself fall, because…"

Lola wanted to steady herself on the railing, but she couldn't move while he held her that hard. She closed her eyes and returned to Beau's arms that night, under the stars where an unexpected love bloomed inside her. She didn't fight the memory. She used it. "I was going

136

to change my entire life for you. It was terrifying and risky, but you made me feel safe. For a few hours, at least."

He rubbed his smooth cheek against hers. She missed the scruff. "I told you if you left Johnny, I'd be here," he said. "And here I am. I think I had to lose you in order to learn the truth."

"What's the truth?"

"This isn't over. I can't take back what I did, but I should've told you everything before you found out that way. When you wouldn't listen, I got angry. I can't seem to figure out how to give up some control without losing it entirely."

Lola opened her eyes. The mountains were indigo shadows that seemed impossibly far away. In the time she'd known Beau, he'd always been very aware—of himself, of her. How could he not have seen the pettiness of what he'd done, the sheer egoism of it? He'd stood to gain real love and a life that centered around something other than work. Instead, he'd thrown it away in the name of pride. That was something she couldn't explain to him, though. It would have to be a lesson learned.

"I can't just pretend nothing happened," Lola said.

"I don't expect you to. I know I have a lot to make up for."

She narrowed her eyes. "So you're willing to try?"

Beau took a mug of coffee and handed it to her. Instead of picking his up, he returned his arm around her. "If you're willing to take it day by day. This is new territory for me, but I'm a fast learner. You know I'll do what it takes to fix it."

Lola did know. If her forgiveness was his prize, then he would make it his. It was an impossible feat, she knew. But he didn't. It would drive Beau even more, sink him in deeper. "When do we start?"

"We already have." It sounded like he was smiling. "I work on Saturdays, but I'll leave it for Monday. You're my queen this weekend."

"And after this weekend?"

"We go home."

"Home?" she asked. "As in…?"

Beau took an arm off her to drink some coffee. "As in you, where I am, when I wake up, when I go to sleep. When I leave for work, when I get back."

Lola felt like she'd eaten cotton. So little time had passed, it was hard not to still want that with Beau—*home*. A life, a future. For him to forgo his work to spend time with her was his highest compliment. But with her wounds so fresh, she was a slave to her pain, and it ran deep. This wasn't a new life with him. It was a chance to be by Beau's side every morning and every night. To get so deep under his skin, he couldn't rid himself of her. To bring down the walls around his heart so she could hold it in her palm, exposed and unprotected. It wouldn't be easy to love the devil, but she could do it if it meant sending him to hell where he belonged.

"I want that too," she said.

"Good. You know I'd get my way even if you didn't."

He was teasing her, so she laughed lightly.

"Now that that's settled," he continued, his voice hardening, "how about enlightening me to your thought process when you left my room yesterday morning."

"Yesterday morning?" Lola took a sip from her mug, stalling. Abrupt, probing inquiries like that needed consideration before answering.

"Warner said you walked home from the hotel."

"That's right. Yes, I did."

"It was still dark." He waited a moment, as if that warranted a response. "Well? What in the hell made you think that was a good idea?"

She squinted out at the skyline. "I had to blow off some steam."

"You couldn't have done that in the back of a car?"

"No." Lola shifted on her feet. There was an edge to both their voices. This was too familiar to them, and they slipped into their battles easily. He'd been putty in her hands for a moment, but she should've known he wouldn't allow that very long. "Why do you ask?"

"I don't know," he said in a tone that conveyed he definitely did know. "Maybe because we were robbed at gunpoint a few hours before that. Correct me if I'm wrong, but it seems like safety would've been pretty high on your list of priorities."

"Does it matter? I made it in one piece." She sniffed. As if he had any right to worry about her after he'd cast her aside so carelessly. "Anyway, I didn't have a choice. I needed to be alone."

"With no cell phone and no credit cards. In the dark." The air around them thickened. "It gets me worked up again just thinking about it."

"Does it?" Lola continued to look forward, carefully tucking it all away for later. His cares, concerns, triggers. "Well, then, it's a good thing I had plenty of cash, thanks to you."

"Are you fucking kidding? People have killed over far less money than what you had in your hands." He removed his arm from her. "Where's that money now?"

Lola turned around and leaned back against the banister. "Downstairs in my room. I fit as much as I could in the safe, but—"

"Jesus Christ, Lola." He jerked his thumb over his shoulder. "That money needs to go in the bank yesterday. You're asking for trouble carrying that kind of cash around."

"You're right." Lola set down her mug and put her arms around his neck. There was no way in hell she was loosening her grip on the one thing keeping her afloat. That money was all she had left. "I'll do it soon."

"Not *soon*. You'll do it Monday. And today, we're getting you a new phone. You can't be without one."

"I don't mind being out of touch, actually." Lola had to stop herself from grinning. Toying with Beau had always been fun, no matter how she'd felt about him. "It's so refreshing to be free from the chains of society for once—"

"I'll stop you right there," Beau said, removing her hands from him by her wrists. "You're getting a phone today. It'll be our first errand. Then we'll see about getting you a temporary credit card until we can get you a real one. I'll give you one of mine too, but you should have a couple in your name just in case—"

"Beau, don't you think you're overreacting a bit—?"

"No. Look at me." Lola lifted her eyes to his and waited. He pulled her hands back to his chest, right over his heart. "Yesterday, even though I thought I'd never see you again, it still drove me insane knowing you were out there with nothing. Don't fight me on this. Without a cell phone or credit card, anything could happen to you, and I wouldn't even know."

Lola's heart jumped into her throat.

"It drove me insane...out there with nothing...I wouldn't even know..."

Beau had reassured her that he never backtracked on his decisions. Never changed his mind. When he wanted something, he took it. Always. But what would happen if the thing he wanted most slipped right through his fingers—and not even his fortune could get it back?

Lola had the motive to bring Beau to his knees, and she had the means to make it happen. All she needed now to complete the puzzle was Beau's heart in her palm.

She stepped even closer to him and looked into his fiery, green eyes. Gently, she twisted her hands out of his grip to reach up and cup his face. And what a face it was—the kind a girl could get lost in if she didn't know any better. "If that's what you want, Beau, then I'll do it. I trust you."

Beau kissed the insides of her hands. Any bitterness left his expression as his features softened.

Beau loved to play—to hunt his prey. That must've been because he'd never lost.

Maybe someone ought to beat him at his own game. Maybe then he wouldn't think it was so fun.

Chapter Sixteen

Present day

Beau wasn't home at seven o'clock for his big surprise date with Lola—he was home earlier. His last meeting had been a homerun despite being distracted and had put him on track to close a lucrative deal. As if he hadn't already been riled thinking of all the things he'd finally get to do to Lola, making money always gave him a buzz. He'd waited her out—not patiently, but he'd waited—and he didn't want to miss a minute of their evening together.

Now, he was perched on their bed while Lola finished getting ready. She came out of the bathroom with a towel wrapped securely under her armpits.

"Come on," Beau said, practically falling off the edge of the mattress. "Just give me a sneak peek."

She smiled. "You only have a few hours left. Your reward will be that much sweeter if you wait."

She'd been stubborn from the start, but Christ did it frustrate him in the best way possible. Night after night, sleeping next to her, sharing a bathroom and a bedroom with her, and she'd only slipped once. He'd been clinging to that memory like a castaway to a raft.

"You're a tough negotiator," Beau said, following her with his eyes until she disappeared into the closet.

"It isn't a negotiation," she called. "You broke the terms of our agreement once. Do it again, and it'll be the last time."

"If you're trying to torture me, it's working. Hearing you talk business gets me even harder."

She leaned out of the closet, giving him a glimpse of her naked shoulder and the outer curve of her breast. "Why? It reminds you of that morning Johnny and I came to your conference room?"

Beau licked his lips. He was as close to having her now as he had been that day. She'd sat across the table from him, statue-like, but once in a while, her face would flicker with hurt or embarrassment when Johnny spoke—or when he was decidedly quiet. All Beau had gotten from her was anger. "Would it upset you if it did?"

"No." She ran her finger along the edge of the doorway. "Maybe one day you can fuck me on that table."

Beau had been teasing about getting hard, but her dirty talk was an alarm to his sleeping cock. Beau resisted standing up. He wasn't sure he could keep himself in check. "Let's skip dinner."

She shook her head. "I've been planning tonight for a while. Besides, I'm *hungry*."

"Give me sixty seconds, and you'll forget the meaning of the word."

"Sixty seconds?" She grinned and returned into the closet. "Is that what I have to look forward to?"

"It would serve you right after keeping me on edge for so long."

A dresser drawer rolled open, then closed with a wooden thump. He was more tempted than ever to sneak in and steal a look at her white breasts and long, tight tummy. He'd showered after work, but already he could use another cold one.

Beau was in love with her, at least he was pretty sure of it, and that feeling was strongest in moments like this one. For a woman who'd worn as many jeans-and-shirt combos in her life as Beau had suits, she was completely at ease in the things he picked out for her. He could just sit and watch, and he never had the urge to walk away. If any other woman had told him 'look don't touch' night after night, Beau would've laughed at her on his way out the door.

Lola came out in a structured black trench coat. "Do you like it?" she asked with a twirl, her high heels' red soles flashing.

She could've been wearing a nun's habit, and he would've said yes. The coat cinched at her waist, all hips and breasts. She'd pulled the collar up around her neck.

It was buttoned all the way, but her long, bare legs invited him to look.

"Can I see the dress?" he asked.

"Not yet." She walked over to the bed, bent over and pressed a light kiss to the corner of his mouth. "Soon."

She straightened up to walk away. He grabbed her wrist, and her head jerked in his direction, her lips splitting apart as if he'd startled her. It took a second, but her mouth spread into some mutation of a smile. She slid her hand through his and walked into the bathroom, promising, "Five more minutes, then we can go."

Five minutes sounded like a lifetime. Anything longer felt impossible. He'd waited long enough for her. From where he sat, he could see her bent over the sink putting in her earrings. Seeing her in that position again made his brain foggy. He could easily fuck her over the bathroom counter before dinner. He wouldn't last long anyway. An appetizer. Then, later, the main course—taking his time unwrapping her, tracing the lines of her curves with his hands and lips.

Beau blew out a sigh. He'd thought he'd been patient their first two nights together by not taking her the moment the sun had set. He'd had no idea what was in store for him.

Lola came out of the bathroom and held her hand out, rescuing both of them from him. "Ready?"

◆ ◆ ◆

Beau raised his wineglass over the table. "To you," he said to Lola.

She made no move to pick up her drink. "Why me?"

"Because there's nothing more worthy of toasting. Unless you have a better idea?"

"Us." She spun the wineglass between her fingers on the tablecloth. "And the end of a very difficult journey."

"That's not how I see it. In a few minutes, my patience over the last few weeks will earn me a great reward."

She grinned. "We are not having sex in a few minutes. We haven't even eaten yet."

Beau sighed. "Fine. A few hours. Whatever. Regardless, tonight isn't an ending. It's the start of a life we've both deserved for a long time."

"To that—exactly." She clinked her wine with his, and they each took a sip. "Thank you for giving Warner the night off like I asked."

"I told you I'd let you plan your night. Brigitte needs the company anyway."

Lola raised her eyebrows. "He's been spending a lot of time at her apartment."

"Someone has to, and it's not going to be me. All my free time goes to someone else."

"Who?" Lola asked. "Because it isn't me."

Beau cleared his throat. He couldn't tell if she was joking. He understood that his schedule bothered her, but what he couldn't comprehend was why. Every day he'd worked the past ten years—and every hour he worked now—was for her, even if he hadn't known it. He went in early and he stayed late to give her more and more and more. "I do my best."

"Do you? She has a point about Warner, you know. If you'd ever sent him home to eat dinner with me because you couldn't make it, I can tell you right now, it would not have gone over well."

Beau put his glass down. "What neither you nor Brigitte seems to get is that if I don't give my job one-hundred-and-ten percent, there'd be no Warner. There'd be no five-thousand square foot house to come home to. No extra bedrooms for a family, no cinema or pool—"

Lola shifted backward in her seat, her eyebrows needling together. "A family?"

Beau maintained eye contact the way he would if he'd slipped up in a meeting. It wasn't like children were at all prevalent in his day-to-day thoughts, but some abstract idea of a family had crossed his mind since Lola had moved in. He leaned his elbows on the table. "I'm making a point."

She looked at her lap. "Have I made you feel like I wouldn't be happy without those things?"

"Which things?"

"A big house and a chauffeur. A closet full of expensive clothing."

He didn't mean to glance at her new coat, but he did. She noticed. "I love the coat on you. I want to give you beautiful things." He was uncomfortable, but she looked at ease. He never knew how to take it when she got angry with him for spending money on her. "Why don't you take it off, show me your new dress? You don't need a coat in here."

"There is no dress."

He looked at her a second longer, then back at the coat. No dress? *One* layer of fabric sat between him and heaven? "You mean…?"

"Has anyone ever told you you're good at changing the subject?"

He pressed his lips together, jolted from the fantasy of what he'd find when he untied her belt, slipped each button open. He backtracked into the argument from the coat to beautiful things to her being possibly— unhappy?

"Lola, it makes me feel good to give you that life. It's a labor of love. Otherwise, what've I worked for all this time?"

After another delicate sip of wine, she said, "You were fine before I came along."

"I was fine." Beau nodded. He reached out, pulled her hand across the table, held it tightly in his. He'd mostly only seen her with nerves of steel, so her clammy palm felt foreign. She still wasn't acting like herself. Perhaps he hadn't given her the comfort she'd needed to do what she was about to do—open up to him again. "Now, I'm not fine. I'm so much more. I'm happy, Lola. Because of you. Because I—"

Lola jerked her hand back and coughed into it. She cleared her throat a couple times and drank water, droplets falling onto the tablecloth. "I'm sorry. It's the wine. It makes my throat dry." She glanced over his shoulder. "Oh, look—our food."

The waiter set down Lola's steak. Beau didn't take his eyes off her, but she examined her plate so hard, he wondered if she was avoiding him.

"Looks delicious," she said. "This place had great reviews."

Beau opened his mouth to finish what he'd been about to say, but she took a bite. He'd be damned if he told her he loved her for the first time while she had a mouthful of tenderloin. He picked up his fork and knife and cut into his T-bone, deciding to wait until later when they were home in bed. He figured there was no better time to tell her than right before she made herself most vulnerable to him.

He continued to watch her as he chewed. He did love her. It wasn't easy for him to say, never really had been, which was why he'd been trying to tell her in other ways. He'd gotten her tickets to the ballet because she'd told him how she'd taken lessons all through her childhood. That, and it was another excuse to take her out, show her off.

They ate silently. Beau didn't mind. The less talking they did, the faster they'd finish and get home. It was all he could do not to rip the fork out of her hand and hurry her to the car.

As soon as Beau had wiped his mouth with his napkin and dropped it on his plate, the waiter appeared. He must've sensed Beau's animal need to get the fuck out of there.

"Can I interest you in any dessert?"

"We're in a hurry."

"I'll bring the check, and…?"

Lola nodded up at him. He inclined his head and walked away. She took a compact mirror from her purse and reapplied her lipstick.

"What was that with the waiter?" Beau asked.

She ran the tip of her index finger along the corner of her mouth, wiped excess gloss on her napkin and shut the compact. "I have something for you."

"Give it to me at home." Beau slid out his chair, stood and buttoned his suit jacket.

She looked up, and a smile spread across her face. Now, she seemed the complete opposite of nervous. "What's the rush?"

"Weeks, Lola. It's been weeks." The waiter headed back toward them with something in his hand. "I'm dying here."

"Sit down, Beau. I promise you'll like your gift."

He unbuttoned his jacket again, ran a hand through his hair and sat. Unless his gift was Lola spread eagle on the restaurant table, he doubted it was worth another few minutes of him not having sex. "All right. Where is it?"

Lola's cheeks turned pink. "It's already here. I wanted it to be a surprise."

The waiter returned to the table and set the check in front of Beau. Next to it, he placed a flat, white box tied with a red ribbon.

Beau tilted his head. "What's this?"

"Your gift."

"I thought it would be—" He stopped. He didn't know what he'd thought, but he hadn't expected it to

151

come in a box. He looked up at her. "I can't believe I didn't think to get you anything."

"There's no better gift you could give me than what will happen tonight. Please, open it."

Beau pulled one end of the bow, and the ribbon fell away. What could it be? He already had plenty of cologne, and an enviable collection of Montblanc pens. The box was the wrong shape for those things anyway. He listed in his head the things Brigitte or ex-girlfriends had bought him over the years—cufflinks, courtside basketball seats, a sterling silver money clip. He lifted the lid.

It took a moment to register what he was looking at. He picked up a headband topped with a pair of jet-black, furry cat ears. Each one had a smaller pink triangle in the center. "What is this?"

"It's what I'm going to wear when I dance for you tonight."

Beau's eyes jumped to hers. "Dance for me? Tonight?"

She nodded. "We've been through a lot. I want to go back to where it all started."

"The only place we're going is home." Beau tossed the ears on the table and scribbled his signature on the check. He leaned across the table toward her but didn't bother lowering his voice. "You think I'll last two minutes watching you dance for me? You'll be lucky if I don't jump across this table and give this entire restaurant a show they'll never forget. My patience is gone, Lola."

"Beau—"

"Tomorrow, I'll lounge on the couch all day long while you twirl around wearing whatever you want on your head. And I'll love every minute of it. But right now, I'm going to fuck the living daylights out of you faster than you can say pussycat."

Lola leveled her eyes on him with a playfulness that hadn't been there before. She ran her tongue along her bottom lip. "Pussycat."

Beau rose from his chair so quickly, it almost toppled over. "We're leaving."

Lola also stood, quietly placing the cat ears back in the box and covering them with the lid. "Our date isn't over. Like I said this morning, I've planned it all out."

"And I appreciate that." Beau took Lola's hand and walked away from the table, pulling her along. "You can tell me all about it on the way home."

He opened the door to the restaurant, ushered her out. One nod, and the valet took off down the sidewalk, remembering Beau and his car without prompting.

Lola yanked her hand from his. He looked back at her as she clutched the box to her chest, her breasts rising and falling. "I didn't wait this long just to have you ruin everything because you can't wait a couple more hours," she said, her face flushed, her words clipped. "Do you have any idea what tonight means to me?"

"Yes. Of course I do." Beau sighed and ran his hands over his face. "I'm going to take my time and appreciate you like I did before. I promise. But I've thought of nothing else since you told me tonight is the night, and I'm at the end of my rope here."

She approached him slowly, as if he truly might pounce. He opened his arms to show her he wasn't angry. He wasn't—just really goddamn horny.

She walked into his embrace, looking down as she played with a button on his shirt. "You've been so patient, but I want to do this one, very special thing for you first. Just one more stop. Can you give me that?"

He rubbed his hands up her back between her shoulder blades. The Lamborghini's engine rumbled as it rounded the corner. "All right, pussycat. You have me in the palm of your hand, you know that? Where are you taking me for our last stop?"

She blinked her almond-shaped blue eyes up to his, and her nose twitched. She looked remarkably feline in that moment. "I already told you. We're going back to where it all began. We're going to Cat Shoppe."

Chapter Seventeen

Beau wasn't easy to catch off guard. The incredulous expression on his face excited Lola—she would've been disappointed by anything else. The Lamborghini's growl, quiet but distinct, was the only sound. It idled at the curb where the restaurant's valet had parked it.

"We're going where?" Beau asked finally, his arms loosening around her.

"Cat Shoppe."

"You're going to wear those," he nodded at the box in her hand with the cat ears, "and dance for me?"

Lola grinned. "Surprised?"

"A little. Yes. That night you want to recreate wasn't exactly our best moment."

"I don't know," Lola said softly, fixated on his shirt button, circling her fingertip over it. "You and I remember it different."

"We do?" His chest rose with his inhalation. "You never mentioned that."

She blinked her lashes up to him again. God, those green eyes, when he focused them on her—a tornado could hit, and she wouldn't even notice. She stopped her fluttering and blinked hard, getting back on track.

She wasn't a liar at heart. With Beau, she'd been dealing words like cards from a deck, checking them close to her chest before setting them down. But this story? She didn't need to edit or tweak it. It was all true.

"A handsome stranger comes in to my shit job and demands to have me all to himself. We flirt. I brush against his leg on purpose, even though we could both get in trouble for that kind of thing." Lola leaned in and nuzzled his Sandalwood-aftershave-scented neck. "While we talk, I think to myself—this is the first time in here I've ever wished a man was just a man. Not a customer. I wonder how I can even bring up the idea of leaving with him without it sounding bad."

He looked down at her. "Is any of that true, or are you just trying to get me to agree to go?"

"Are you agreeing?"

"I had no idea you felt that way."

He would've if he'd asked, but he hadn't. She dropped her hand from his chest. "I did. I liked you. But I know that night was awful for you, and that's why I want to replace it with this one. That's your gift."

"I don't want to replace that night. I loved everything about it right up until you turned me down." Beau put his knuckle under her chin and ghosted his thumb across her bottom lip. "And we wouldn't be here right now if it hadn't happened."

Lola almost moved away from him—it never got easier, hearing him say the things she deserved to hear. But Beau was nothing if not observant when it came to her. One misstep, and he'd suspect something was wrong.

He turned first, opening the Lamborghini's passenger-side door for her. "Coming?"

She stood in place a moment, collecting herself. His spell was strong tonight—or maybe she was getting nostalgic. She could call everything off, and he'd be none the wiser. Go home, give in to the love she'd been fighting, let him take from her what he wanted. And take, take, take, always without consequence.

She got in the car. On their way to Cat Shoppe, he took her hand in his as he sometimes did when he drove. She doubted he even realized it. Like the time he'd found her in the Four Seasons lounge and wrapped her jaw in his hand. By his firm grip and unforgiving tone, he'd meant to be threatening, but he'd gently rubbed his thumb against her skin. As Beau's guard lowered, his body language became easier to read every day.

Lola glanced over at him. And every day he somehow got more handsome. Once or twice, at night, when he'd assumed she was asleep, she'd peeked at him poring over his laptop, sheets of paper all over the comforter. He'd said bringing his work to bed was a new thing for him, but either he did it there next to her or alone in his study. It was a sweet threesome—her, him and his mistress, the Bolt Ventures quarterly report.

Then, in the morning, they'd wake up together, even if she wasn't getting out of bed. Without fail, he'd lean over and whisper hotly in her ear, "Shower with me." Lola knew better than that, though. She'd been strong so far, but she wasn't made of steel.

"What's wrong?" Beau asked.

Lola blinked several times, clearing the haze of her thoughts. "What?"

He looked at her from the driver's side. "You've been staring at me."

"Oh." She sat back in her seat. "I was just thinking about how this is our last night like this."

"Like what?"

Out the windshield, Hollywood's bright lights blurred, stars pinholed the dark sky. She'd given so much thought to the details of their date that she hadn't had time to consider the next morning. What would he do?

"Never mind," she said. "In case I forget, I did laundry today, but I didn't get a chance to fold it. It's in the dryer." She picked at her fingernail. "And I moved the glasses and bowls back into their own cabinet."

"But you like them with their matching dishes."

"No, you were right. It makes more sense to sort them by type. It's your kitchen, after all."

Beau laughed harmoniously, squeezed her hand and brought it to his lips. "Relax." He pressed a quick kiss to her knuckles. "Don't be nervous. You already know how this goes."

She tilted her head in his direction. "Do I?"

"I'll do the work. I already know every single thing I'm going to do to you tonight. You just get to enjoy the ride."

He looked back at the road, but she studied his profile. Once in a while, it took all her strength to remember how she'd gotten here. It'd been a dewy Friday morning before most of the city had been awake. He'd crushed her without mercy. He'd ripped away something she'd finally let herself have—hopes and dreams for an extraordinary future with him. He was beautiful, and she loved him, but the only thing that would ease the constant throb of her broken heart was his suffering.

Lola was closing in on him. At the dinner table, she'd sensed he'd been about to tell her he loved her. It was the validation she'd been hoping for, but she'd interrupted him, suddenly terrified that if he said it, she wouldn't be able to go through with tonight.

She didn't need to hear it anyway. She already knew he loved her—she just wanted him to know it too. If he didn't, he would soon.

"Enjoy the ride?" she whispered to herself. "I think I will."

❖ ❖ ❖

Typical for a Friday night, Sunset Boulevard was clogged with traffic. It was a small detail that hadn't crossed Lola's mind, but as they crept down the street toward Cat Shoppe, then passed it, her spine lengthened.

"What're you doing?" she asked Beau.

He flipped on his blinker, waiting for the cars in front of them to move. "Parking around back. There weren't any spots on the street, and I don't have the patience to wait for one."

Her throat went dry. The first time he'd brought her here, he'd slid into a front spot. That was how she'd envisioned this going, and it could pose a problem later. She craned her neck, praying for an open spot. "You don't want to leave your car in back."

"Why not?"

She adjusted her buttoned-up collar, already dampening with sweat. The air was cool, but it suddenly seemed fucking stupid to have worn a coat she couldn't take off until they were alone. "Shady characters. There's, like, no lights in the parking lot. A car like this won't last five minutes."

He laughed as traffic opened up, allowing him to turn onto a side street that led to the back. "There're lots of people out tonight. It'll be fine."

She rubbed her hairline. If she pushed it, he'd ask her why it mattered to her. She'd just have to work around it.

Beau pulled into a spot and shut off the car. They sat there for an unusually still moment, a dreamlike state, Lola still not sure she could pull this off. Maybe if she didn't move, she wouldn't have to. She shook her head quickly to shoo the ridiculous thought. This was what she'd wanted for weeks, and she wasn't turning back now.

Beau looked at her in the dark. "Thank you."

"For what?" she asked, keeping her eyes forward.

He reached over and turned her head to him. He leaned in, pulling her closer by her chin, and kissed her once on the lips. "Sometimes I forget how it feels to receive a gift without a price tag. I know you put a lot of thought into this."

"I did." Lola forced herself not to look away. Was he just figuring out that what made something special was the thought behind it, not the dollar amount? Sporadic comments like those made her think Beau was changing in little ways, that maybe he wouldn't always put money and work first. She hoped he'd keep going down that path. "There's something else."

"More?"

Lola removed the lid from the box in her lap and held up the cat ears. "As soon as I put these on my head, I'm no longer your girlfriend. I'm a stranger. A— sex worker."

The corner of his mouth crooked into a smile. He dropped his hand to one of her thighs, squeezing it right under the hem of her coat. "Is it bad if that excites me?"

Lola removed his hand by his wrist and placed it back on his side of the car. "That means absolutely no touching tonight. You're getting an authentic experience. You're my customer, and you've hired me to dance for you, just like you did that first night. Which means keeping your hands to yourself."

Beau sighed up at the roof. "I've come this far—what's a little longer?" He looked back over at her. "Anything else, my queen?"

No—there was nothing else. Except that she couldn't seem to move from that spot and get out of the car. He was being so good tonight. Attentive. A real boyfriend—better than Johnny, even better than Beau at his best. "Yes," she said softly. "Kiss me."

Beau put his hand to her cheek without hesitation. He inclined over the console and brushed the tip of his nose against hers. He pecked her once, but she put her arms around his neck before he could pull away. They opened their mouths to each other at the same time, their warm tongues meeting in the middle. It wasn't in her plan. It wasn't even her parting gift to him. This one was just for her.

He inhaled and separated from her but kept his forehead pressed against hers. "You sure you don't want to just go home?"

She hesitated to seem genuine, but she was ready. She was picturing ahead to being inside, dancing close to him, turning him raw and defenseless. She lifted the cat ears on her index finger and dangled them in front of him. "Want to do the honors?"

He took the headband and placed it over her hair. "Perfect."

Beau got out and rounded the car to get her door. He held out a hand to help her, but she shook her head at him.

"Right," he said, dropping it back to his side. "No touching."

She unfolded out of the Lamborghini, and they walked around to the front, shoulder to shoulder.

The bouncer took one look at Lola and opened the velvet rope for them. "Evening, Miss Winters."

"You really went all out, didn't you?" Beau asked behind her.

She ignored him and passed through the entryway into the club. The music hit her like a fist to the gut, uglier than usual, all hard bass without any detectable rhythm. Or maybe her brain was jumbling things that didn't matter, unable to afford the extra attention. Kincaid was at the bar, watching over things like he sometimes did. Neon streaks cut through the dark like they were trying to dismember him. They exchanged a nod.

"Follow me," she said to Beau over her shoulder. She was in charge for once. That was how she knew she had Beau. He was letting her get away with more than he would anyone else, especially tonight.

She walked him down a long hallway until they reached the last door. There, Lola took a moment to herself. With a deep breath, she adjusted her headband and smoothed her hand over her trench coat. What had Kincaid called her earlier that day?

"The cat that swallowed the canary."

She liked that. She'd have to remember it.

Lola opened the door and led Beau into their final moments together.

Chapter Eighteen

Cat Shoppe's VIP room was more than familiar to Lola and Beau. After all, this would be their third time renting it.

"VIP?" Beau asked from behind her as they entered.

"It was either here or out there," Lola teased, nodding toward the main stage.

Beau stepped so close to her, she felt his heat on her back. "You don't think I'd let you dance out there, where anyone could see. Do you?"

Lola walked deeper into the room to get away from him. Just being back there, remembering how she'd gotten to her knees and sucked him off, was enough to make her heart beat a little faster. She gestured toward the red-velvet couch, which curved around the circular room. "Sit."

He obeyed, easing into the seat, looking amused as he crossed an ankle over his knee. "If I'm the customer, aren't I in charge?"

"If it makes you feel better to think so." Lola took her time unknotting the belt of her trench coat. "Sometimes I'm not sure which one of us is in charge—but I guess that's just the dynamic of our relationship, isn't it?"

He wasn't listening. His eyes were fixed on her hands as she slid each button through its slit. Appreciating her, that was what he liked. Owning her body, even from a distance. The poor man hadn't even seen her tits since the night she'd fled his hotel room.

She removed the seventeen-hundred dollar trench coat and let it fall on the ground.

His foot slipped, and he planted it on the floor, leaning his elbows onto his legs. "Fuck. Lola."

"I'm not Lola in here." This wasn't just about revenge. Beau wasn't the only one who could have fun. Her real name would be a clue, but he was so distracted, he would miss it. "I go by Melody."

She stared at him, staring at her. He didn't move or even blink, but he didn't look particularly happy either. For the first time, she noticed how quiet the room was except for the bass thumping from the main stage.

She glanced down quickly, checking her outfit—could she have forgotten an important part? The Swarovski-studded corset pushed her breasts up, plump and smooth. Where the hem stopped, a black, lacey thong started and attached to matching, thigh-high stockings. The ears had come with a black cattail she'd haphazardly pinned to her underwear in the restaurant's bathroom.

He still hadn't reacted. She tried not to fidget. "Do you like it?"

He cocked his head, stabbing his tongue into his cheek. "It's the same thing you wore that night."

"Is that a yes?"

He rubbed his hands over his face without removing his eyes from her. "I don't know. It makes me think of how you used to dance here. And the other men who came before me."

Lola shifted from one foot to the other. The point was to trigger his memory, to make him crazy for her. Jealousy was an unexpected reaction. "It was a long time ago."

"So? Those men looked at something they had no right to." His eyes were dark and narrowed when he finally looked up at her face. "They sat here. They thought about you when they got home. They're animals. They're—"

"They're *you*." Lola took a breath. There was too much bitterness in her voice, and *he* wasn't supposed to get to *her*. "You were one of them."

"I was not." He shook his head and blinked a few times, hard.

Lola tried to keep her limbs loose when all she wanted to do was tense up. This was not going as she'd hoped. "What are you saying?"

They stared at each other. If he got up to leave, she might not be able to stop him. It took a great deal to distract a man like Beau—she'd hoped two-and-a-half weeks of keeping his hands to himself would be enough.

He glanced behind her briefly and back. "I don't know. I can't think straight when you're standing there in that." His eyebrows lowered. "Take it off."

Her body thrilled. He was giving her the green light. This was the Beau she'd been anticipating. She traced her finger along the corset's sweetheart neckline. "And if I don't?"

"Then I'll do it for you. I wanted tonight to be special, but you want to get bent over in a filthy strip club? I'm game, baby. It'll be just as sweet for me anywhere I fuck you."

Lola flushed all at once, as if she'd swallowed a ball of fire. She was back in his hotel room, crawling to him across the floor, the opposite of mad about it. Staying apart had been hard for her too. There were times she'd wanted nothing more than to give in to his advances, let him pleasure her the way she already knew he could.

"Remember what I said outside. I'm serious." Lola turned away from him. She had to be careful. Nothing made her knees quiver faster than Beau at the end of his patience, nothing on his mind but how to get inside her.

She crouched to slip an iPod from the pocket of her trench coat, then plugged it into the stereo. Jazz started slow, sensual. *Fever* was something you wanted when Shirley Horn sang about it in her smoky, hypnotic voice.

Lola got on the round stage, a pole down the center, the same one she'd danced on for him before. Tonight, the room didn't turn colors—there was just a single, white spotlight from the ceiling that illuminated her and shaded him.

Lola looked down at her feet and took a couple deep breaths, exhaling each one slowly. She glanced up at him. Her lashes were heavy with mascara, a black shadow over Beau. She hadn't even begun, and her chest already rose and fell rapidly. She did love to dance, especially for Beau, because she felt him in her every move. He could direct her without a word or touch.

She took the pole, cold and solid, and started in a slow circle. Her resolve strengthened each time her heels hit the compact floor. She slid her palm high up the smooth surface, grabbed the pole with both hands. She jumped it like a boyfriend she hadn't seen in years, swinging with her legs locked around it. The furry cattail belted her thigh.

Beau flexed his large hands over his knees. "Come here."

Still suspended from the pole, with both hands gripping the metal, Lola arched her back. Her hair cascaded behind her. She lowered herself to her feet and turned away from him, zigzagging her hips as she danced into a squat. Watching him, she zigzagged back up.

His eyes followed her every movement. He looked like he'd forgotten how to swallow. "I surrender. You've got me. Just come down here."

"Patience," she said, turning to face him. With a hint of a smile, she unhooked her corset just enough to free everything above her nipples. "This isn't about satisfaction. It's about torment."

169

"It's about me climbing on that stage in two seconds and nailing you to that pole."

Lola practically purred her assent, her insides turning to jelly with his tone. This was working even faster than she'd expected. She descended the steps steadily, keeping her eyes down, and went to stand between his parted knees. She turned slowly. Lola liked to feel free when she danced, but she forced her hips to stay with the tempo. Beau would pick up her cues, staying slow along with her.

He grabbed her tail. She turned her head over her shoulder and tsked at him.

He smiled a little and let go. "You have no idea, do you?"

"What?"

"How it's been for me." His face fell. "How fucking badly I've needed you."

"It's been like that for me too," Lola said, still twisted to see his eyes, still dancing.

"Has it? Sometimes I don't know."

Lola faltered but didn't stop. These moments of clarity he kept having weren't helping. She hadn't anticipated anything from him other than consuming, dumb lust. "I don't know what you mean."

"You still have a wall up, and I can't blame you for that. But I'll break it down with every last tool I have. I'm doing the work, Lola. Even if you can't see it all the time."

She swallowed. The finality of it all began to sink in. Once upon a time, Lola and Beau had made a plan to spend all their nights together. Now, they didn't even have one left. It was another thing Beau had taken away—this was *his* fault, not hers. He had ruined this.

"Don't call me that," she said, angry. "I told you. It's Melody."

Beau raked a hand through his hair, disheveling its perfection. "Would you stop moving a minute?"

"You ordered me to dance."

"Well, now I'm ordering you to stop."

Lola stilled her hips and looked at the floor. She'd spent the last three weeks studying him. Learning him inside out. Handling him. She could do this. She turned to face him.

"I—" He paused and took a breath.

Lola's heart began to race. There was no way he'd tell her he loved her *here* of all places. In the middle of a striptease. Part of her wanted to hear it, but the part that wanted to leave was stronger.

She climbed onto the cushion and straddled him with her knees, careful not to touch him.

"I should've stopped this already," he said. "I don't want to do this here."

Lola lowered her voice to a sultry whisper. "Then where do you want to do it?"

"At home. In our bed."

She couldn't resist getting a little closer. He smelled like the man who'd uttered nothings in her ear—who'd made love to her while he'd fucked her. But her love for him had torn through her like a hurricane too many times, trying to bring her down. She gripped the cushion behind his shoulders and steeled herself against the urge to give in to him.

She glanced at his lap. "You're hard, Beau. Do you want me?"

He groaned. "On your knees, on your stomach, on your back. Every way. Any way."

She almost sucked in a breath, wanting that too, but she only needed to be strong a little longer. She opened her mouth and finally said what she'd been thinking for weeks. "Your hands are the only ones that ever lit a fire under my skin. God, Beau. I dream about you touching me at night, and I fantasize about it during the day."

"I want to," he said. "I need to."

"I'm right here."

"You made me promise…"

She inhaled his scent, committing it to memory along with the things that were already there—his foggy-green eyes, his razorblade jawline and sexy cleft chin. His thawing embrace. "It's too much. You told me once, when you fucked me, it would calm me. I can't even see straight."

He grabbed her by the waist, making her gasp, and pulled her onto him. He yanked her thong out of the way and sank a finger in her.

Lola threw her head back, bit her lip to keep quiet and looked directly into the surveillance camera. She didn't expect the second finger, and she moaned gutturally.

"There's my girl," Beau said.

There was an eruption, and Lola looked back just as the door bounced off the wall. Beau was still gawking, knuckles deep inside her when she was hauled backward off his lap.

Beau's hands were suspended, open and empty. "What—"

A security guard seized his bicep, pulling Beau to his feet. "You're out, pal."

"Get your hands—" Beau jerked his arm away. "Don't touch me."

The man's muscles, as big as Lola's head, stretched the sleeves of a faded-black T-shirt. His face reddened. "Exactly. Did you miss the huge fucking sign out there that says '*no touching*'?"

"She's my *girlfriend*," Beau said, his voice as sharp-cornered as his back was rigid.

Another security guard entered the room and got between Lola and Beau. "You good, Havermann?"

Beau laughed like a shotgun, short, aggressive barks. "Is this some kind of joke?"

"No joke," the man called Havermann said. He reached up but stopped as Beau raised his hands, a warning to back off. "You don't touch the girls. Everyone knows that. Automatic removal. Let's go. Now."

Beau looked between Lola and the man too quickly to even register her. "She's not one of your girls. She's mine, and I don't like how you're blocking her from me," he said to Havermann. "Get the fuck out of my way. Lola, tell them."

Lola opened her mouth. *I have to settle the bill. I'll meet you out front.* She froze, unable to get the words out.

Havermann moved, obstructing Beau almost completely from Lola's sight. "Don't worry about her. You got another concern right now—me. Get out, or I put you out."

"Beau, go," Lola said suddenly, trying to shuffle around Havermann. She didn't want it to get physical. "I'll meet you out front."

"And leave you here alone?" Beau lurched from side to side to see her better. "Are you out of your mind?"

The other security guard crossed his arms. "You got three seconds."

Lola bit her thumbnail. "Go ahead. I know these guys. I just have to settle the bill, and get my things—"

"I'll buy you new things."

One of the men grunted. "Three."

Her heart pounded as she hesitated. "I'll only be a minute—"

"Two."

"Did you not hear what I said?" Beau snapped. "So help me God, Lola. Leave your shit, and let's fucking go. *Now.*"

Havermann's chest swelled. "I'm not letting her leave with you. Not when you talk to her like that." He lunged for Beau's arm. "Come—"

Havermann stumbled when Beau stepped back. "Put your hand on me again, I'll break every bone in it."

"You got a fucking death wish?" Havermann grabbed Beau's lapel and yanked, but Beau was faster. He already had two fistfuls of Havermann's SECURITY shirt as he threw him backward into a wall. Beau pulled

Havermann forward and slammed his body a second time. "I don't think you understand."

Lola covered her open mouth. She was as afraid of his expression as she was of him taking on two security guards. "Beau—"

"I've been this way for weeks," Beau said through gritted teeth. "I'm on the edge, and in two seconds, you're going to know exactly what that means. I'm holding back because jail is the only place I'll be worse off."

The other security guard pulled Beau off by the back of his suit. "All right, ladies, enough."

Beau was breathing hard. He stared Havermann down as he was dragged away, then looked pointedly at Lola. "Let's go."

Havermann regained his footing, pinching at his shirt like it was a fine suit. "Just get the fuck out. She said she'll meet you in front. You got to cool off before we leave her alone with you."

"Jesus Christ. She's my goddamn girlfriend."

"Yeah, we heard you." Each of the men took an arm, forcing Beau out of the room.

Lola stood frozen to the spot, her blood rushing, her head spinning like she'd spent the last two minutes running in circles. She held her hands out for balance, worried she'd have to sit, and she didn't have time to sit. It could've gotten violent. But it hadn't. It hadn't, it wouldn't, and it wasn't her problem anyway. She didn't deserve to be the one coming to Beau's defense when the pain he'd inflicted on her was worse than any fist to the stomach.

She flinched with her entire body and snatched her trench coat off the floor. She got it on, throwing the belt into a knot, and stopped at the door. Her plan had worked. Not as smoothly as she'd hoped, but it had—and this? This was the easy part. Walk away. Let go, so everything else could take course. Her dignity, her power—they were there for the taking. She just had to walk away.

She looked down the hall, the way they'd come. It was quiet. Her steps were brisk but her strides long as her memory guided her to Cat Shoppe's backdoor. When Lola had worked there, she and the other girls would slip outside between numbers, leaving a heel in the doorway so they wouldn't get locked out. Lola yanked on the handle, but it didn't budge. Her heart, already racing, began to hammer.

"Damn it," she whispered, pulling it with all her weight. Stuck like a mouse in a cage. There was only one other way out, and Beau was waiting there. She could picture him, a fuming bull, eyes squinted and nostrils flared, his urges pinballing between mowing the place down with his car, breaking Havermann's arms and fucking through his rage.

"Sometimes it sticks," Lola heard from behind her.

Lola whirled around. Marilyn, the bartender-stripper she'd met earlier that day, stood three feet away in her white, vinyl bikini and blonde wig. Lola cleared her throat. "I, um—need a cigarette."

"You don't got to explain. I heard some of what you said to Kincaid today. He hurt you, that guy you came in with?"

"Not like you think."

Marilyn nodded as though she'd heard it a hundred times. "I've been there." She reached over and jerked the handle upward, throwing herself into the door. "There you go," she said as it opened. "We've got to help each other out, right? Some of us really got nobody."

Lola exhaled an unsteady but relieved breath. Something about Marilyn struck her as trustworthy. Maybe it was that no matter how Lola dressed or did her makeup, she'd always have some of the Cat Shoppe girl in her.

Lola reached out and hugged her. They each went completely stiff. For the first time, Lola realized how far she'd gone to sterilize her heart for Beau—it was extending outside of their relationship now.

"Please, don't mention this to anyone," Lola said.

Marilyn shouldered her way out of the embrace, a tight-lipped but sincere smile on her face. She pinched her fingertips together and slid them across her closed mouth. "Our secret."

Lola leaned outside, peering into the dark. It took her eyes a moment to adjust. The backdoor closed and latched, swallowing the club's music. There wasn't time to spare, she knew that. Beau's car sat at the edge of the lot, and she tried to make out the driver's seat. It looked empty.

She took off the cat ears and walked toward his Lamborghini, passing her thumb back and forth over the fur band. Something scurried across her path, and she stopped short, clamping a hand over her mouth to keep herself from screaming. She inhaled a breath and continued to the driver's side.

Beau was smart. Cunning. He would figure out why she'd left, but not at first. She needed to leave something behind so he'd understand she'd made this choice. Otherwise, he might involve the cops. And she didn't need that. She twisted the Lamborghini's side mirror up, kissed the glass and hung the cat ears on it.

She pulled her coat tighter around her body and strode toward an alley, glancing over her shoulder before she entered. The only light came from a Thai restaurant's illuminated sign at the other end. She'd been eating there for years. When she exited the alley, she waved through the window.

The owner met her out front with a plastic bag of hot food and a single key. Lola handed him a fifty, waving off the change. "Thanks for keeping an eye on it."

Directly in front of the building was a car, but not just any car. It was a brand new, violently-red Lotus Evora she'd purchased that afternoon—in cash. She slipped into the driver's seat—the fresh, unbroken leather giving her a noisy welcome—and put the key in the ignition. It was easy—all she had to do was turn it, and she was home free.

Lola had been dealing with men since she was a teenager. They weren't difficult creatures. Beau was in love with Lola. And Lola knew as early as six years old, when her father had left, that your first broken heart was also your most painful. That was what she wanted for Beau. It was simple but effective—moving something he loved just outside his grasp was enough to drive him to the edge. Because one thing was for sure about a man who already owned anything money could buy—the only things left to want were the ones he couldn't have.

They were both getting what they deserved. Her, a chance to start over and find peace, and him—nothing. They couldn't both win the game. She had to choose herself over Beau.

Lola started the car. She didn't have to go by Cat Shoppe on her way, but it would be her only glimpse of victory, even if it was through her black-tinted windows. She looped around and waited for a lull in traffic, then drove by the flashing, neon *Girls* sign. Beau paced the sidewalk, his eyes glued to Cat Shoppe's front door. Had he understood, while being escorted out against his will, how little control he really had? Had he started to realize yet just how much he'd lost?

Lola turned her eyes back to the road, pressed her high heel to the gas pedal and gunned it.

She was out of town within half an hour.

Chapter Nineteen

Tick.
Tick.
Tick.

Beau didn't remove his eyes from Cat Shoppe's front door except to check his Rolex. Seconds slid by in a steady rhythm until almost ten minutes had passed. The bouncer sat on a stool, watching Beau pace like a caged tiger. He'd been instructed to remain twenty feet from the entrance.

"I just want my girlfriend so I can get the fuck out of here," Beau said across the sidewalk.

"Any closer, and you're leaving here in cuffs. Like I said, security didn't take too kindly to your attitude."

Beau pulled his wallet from his suit jacket. "A hundred bucks if you get her out here for me."

The bouncer remained slumped on his seat, chewing gum like it was his job. After a few seconds, he shifted to unclip a radio from his belt. "What's she look like?"

"We arrived together. Black hair, tall."

He globed a hand in front of his chest. "I mean the titties—big? Small?"

Beau glared. "Fuck you. That's my girlfriend."

"Hey, I don't mind the small ones. More of an ass man myself." He chuckled, held the receiver to his mouth. "You got a read on the chick in the kitten ears?" He winked at Beau.

Of course the doorman had noticed Lola, her black Burberry trench and red pout. He had a heartbeat, didn't he? Beau tugged at the ends of his shirtsleeves, though what he really wanted to do was push them up, knock the fucker out along with the rest of the men in that place. They stood between Beau and something that was his. He would've barged back in to get to her, but that'd either land him in a hospital or a jail cell, and then he'd be leaving Lola alone with brutes. He wiped sweat from his hairline, an all too familiar feeling settling in him as the image of Lola with a gun under her chin flashed by.

The radio shrieked with static. "It's Kincaid. That was Lola Winters, worked here back in the day. We checked everywhere. She's gone."

They looked at each other. Beau took a step closer. "Gone?"

"You sure, boss?" the man asked. "She didn't come out this way."

The LED *Girls* sign by the door burned into Beau's retinas. He rubbed his eyes with stiff fingers, searched the sidewalk. The street was busy with cars. A group of people passed by, looking at him, none of them even remotely familiar—as if he'd exited the strip club onto another planet.

Beau took out his phone, his adrenaline spiking when he saw that neither of his last two text messages to Lola had gone through.

"She ain't in here," Kincaid said. "Must've gone out the back."

"There's a backdoor?" Beau started toward the corner.

"Yo—what about my money?" the doorman called after him.

Beau broke into a jog, shouldering through a human cluster. Lola'd definitely promised to meet him out front. Had she needed a quick exit from security? Coming here had been a bad idea. Parking in back, where she was probably waiting in the dark, was a bad idea.

His Lamborghini was in an end spot, close to the street. The only light was a distant sidewalk lamp. Not a person in sight. He looked in the passenger's side window. He got onto his hands and knees to check underneath. She wasn't there, or behind a nearby dumpster, or in the next building's parking lot. He went to the backdoor and pulled on the handle, banged on the metal slab.

He called her. A black shadow near the driver's side door caught his eye—something hanging from the side mirror. He got closer, bending to see it better.

After three melodic beeps over the line, he heard, *"We're sorry, you have reached a number that has been disconnected or is no longer in service. If you feel you have reached this recording in error—"*

Beau ended the call and picked up Lola's black kitten ears. On the glass was a red lipstick mark in the shape of a kiss. He looked between the headband and the mirror. The ears had been on her head. She'd been wearing red lipstick. Had Lola been outside at some point in the last fifteen minutes?

He looked up suddenly. "Lola?" he called, her name fading instantly. "This isn't funny. It's not safe out here."

He turned in a circle. It *wasn't* funny, but no part of him thought this was a joke. The strip club had been busy, but he hadn't noticed a single person. Not one except her. That didn't mean someone hadn't noticed them. He tried to picture a face, anyone's face, or something out of the ordinary. The only thing he saw was Lola's back as she'd led him to the VIP room.

He clutched the cat ears. He'd let security separate them. He shouldn't've left her side, not without a fight. Someone might've hurt her, drugged her, taken her somewhere.

He turned and kicked the dumpster. A metallic thud echoed around the lot, reminding him how empty it was. He paced the sidewalk, rubbing his temples. *Think, think, think.* He was used to remaining calm during a crisis, but his thoughts jumbled. His palms sweat. Her phone was disconnected—how long did that take? Could it be done in—? He checked his watch. Eighteen minutes?

He beat the door with his fist until his palm began to throb, and finally, it cracked open with a heavy click. An older man peered at him. "What?"

"Where is she?"

"I told you already." The man spit chewing tobacco on the sidewalk next to Beau's feet. "She ain't in here."

"She has to be. She's not out here." Beau took a threatening step closer. "You know her?"

The man just looked him over. "Yeah. I'm the owner, Kincaid."

"So what the fuck happened tonight?"

"Not my business. You take that up with her." He went to shut the door, but Beau grabbed it, stopping it cold. Kincaid was short and squat, not nearly as meaty as the security guards.

"Tell me, or I'll get LAPD here within five minutes. I know the chief. You don't want them sniffing around."

He shrugged. "Call them. I got nothing to hide. Maybe you ought to get the police on the phone anyway, because like I said ten times already, your girl isn't in here. And I tell you, I got a real thing about possessive boyfriends. Don't like them, don't want them hanging around. Kind of a pet peeve I got."

Beau didn't remove his hand from the door. He didn't know the police chief personally, but he had a solid link to him. He wasn't going to involve him, though, not yet anyway. He'd had a neighbor call the police on him once, when he and Brigitte had lived in a dump with thin walls, and she'd gotten hysterical over something. The officer'd arrived to find her calm and charming, and by the time he'd left, it was with her phone number. The police had done nothing for Beau that day or since, and they certainly wouldn't give a fuck about a woman who'd gone missing from a strip club twenty minutes ago.

"All right," Beau said, lining up his options. "Okay. What do you want? Money?"

Kincaid reeled slowly back, as if Beau'd offered him a bag of shit. "I want you to get the fuck off my property. That's all we been telling you since the moment you touched her."

"Just tell me why. Why'd you kick me out?"

Kincaid sighed, looked around the lot. "Something fishy here, but if it'll get you to leave, I'll tell you. Lola was here this afternoon, said she was bringing you by, said if you touched her, I should remove you. Treat you like any other customer, but I'll be honest, the guys went easy on you. Weren't really sure what we were dealing with."

Beau breathed through his nose, trying, failing, to put the pieces together. She'd arranged it beforehand, that he'd known, but why go through everything she did, from warning him not to touch her to begging him to? "If I find out she's in there—"

"She ain't. She got a key to your place?"

"Of course."

"Probably at home then. Good luck." Kincaid pulled on the door, and Beau released it. He fumbled with his keys, got into his car and sat with his hands gripping the wheel. He shut his eyes and envisioned himself at the head of his boardroom faced with a problem. Everyone around the table, looking to him for the solution. Because there was an answer. He just needed to find it.

Beau was no angel—he had enemies. Powerful ones. Business was their battlefield. It'd never crossed into personal territory for him—but perhaps he'd pissed off the wrong person.

Beau opened his eyes and looked into the side mirror again, the lip mark plastered on his reflection. It seemed like a message that had nothing to do with business. It was a stretch, thinking someone had targeted Lola to get back at him. Those weren't the kind of enemies he'd made, and Lola wasn't a damsel in distress.

Beau tried her cell again and got the same recording. He turned his phone over in his hand, checked the screen and battery. He dialed Warner as it occurred to him Lola might've contacted him for a ride.

Beau spoke as soon as the line clicked. "Warner, have you heard from—"

"—reached the voicemail of—"

He hung up. Of all the days he could've given Warner off. He called the house, reasoning if Lola had left right after he'd seen her, she could be back there by now, but nobody answered.

There was only one other place she could be, and the last place he wanted to go. He started the car, the engine waking up like a hungry lion. As he pulled out of the parking lot, he made another call.

"Hey Joe." It was a man, not difficult to figure out which one.

Beau cursed silently. He wasn't about to ask Lola's ex-boyfriend if he'd seen her. Lola had talked about two other people she'd worked with, Amanda, who'd blown Johnny, and Veronica, a friend.

"Hello?" Johnny asked.

"I'm calling for Veronica."

"One sec. Vero!"

Beau waited through some shuffling until a woman came on the line. "Yeah?" she asked, already wary.

"Is this Veronica?"

"Who is this?"

"I'm looking for Lola Winters. Have you seen her tonight?"

Veronica grunted. "She doesn't work here anymore."

"Have you seen her, though? Tonight? Is she there now?"

"Now? I haven't seen her since—"

"Who is that?" Beau heard in the background, Johnny again.

"Nobody," Vero said. There was more rustling on the line. "Johnny, what—mind your own fucking business."

"Sounds like my business," he said.

"It's not. Go pour a drink or something."

Beau was halfway between Hey Joe and Cat Shoppe now. He didn't want to go in if he didn't have to. No good would come from being in the same room with Johnny.

"You still there?" Veronica asked after a few silent seconds.

"You haven't seen her since when?" Beau asked.

"Since before she and Johnny broke up. I heard she was with you."

Beau glanced out his window. "You know who I am?"

"You have a way of sticking out. How come you're calling here asking for her when you know she don't work here?"

"You're sure she's not there? If she is, I need to talk to her. It's important."

"I'd tell you if she were. I love her to death, that's why I never want to see her in here again. She don't belong."

Beau frowned. He wouldn't like that either, Lola going to Hey Joe if she were in trouble. "If you see her, tell her to call me. It's important."

"You said that already." She sighed into the phone. "Look, I have to go. Johnny's giving me the death stare."

"Don't mention this to him."

"I won't. My loyalty left the building with Lola once I found about Amanda."

Lola must not've talked to her about Beau, then. Veronica would've certainly shared her opinion of him if she had. Beau stopped mid-Boulevard and flipped the car around. "Thanks for your help," he said and hung up.

Lola was out there, alone, in the dark. He couldn't remember if she'd taken her purse inside. He leaned over to the passenger's side as he drove, feeling around, then did the same in the backseat. No purse. At least she had that, unlike the morning she'd walked home from the Four Seasons. His heart palpitated the same way it had that day, when he'd realized he had no way of getting ahold of her.

Beau was driving in the direction of his house, but he had no idea if it was the right place to be. His phone rang, and he grabbed it without even checking the screen. "Lola?"

"Sorry I missed your call, sir."

"Warner." Beau shut his eyes briefly, a current of dread running through him. "Is Lola with you?"

Warner hesitated. "Is she supposed to be?"

"I can't find her. She disappeared in the middle of our date. I was hoping she'd called you to pick her up."

"No, sir. I haven't heard from her. Have you tried the house?"

Three weeks earlier, when she'd walked out of his life, *she'd* found *him*. Maybe she was already at home. He'd heard when it came to a missing person, it was best to stay in one place so they could find you "Not yet."

"Maybe she took a—one minute." His voice went distant. "Yes, it is. Something about Lola going missing. Just let me—"

"If that's Brigitte," Beau said, "I don't have time. Just let me know if you hear from Lola." Beau hung up, more confident that he'd walk in the front door and find Lola in the kitchen, eating spoonfuls of Rocky Road from the carton the way she sometimes did.

He made it home in record time, parking in the driveway and jogging up to the front. He dropped his keys, cursed as he picked them up, and finally got the door open. The house was dark.

"Lola?" he called out, flipping the switch for the chandelier. He tossed his keys on the table and headed through the house, turning on a light in every room. As he entered the kitchen, he prayed for the glow of the refrigerator, the sound of silverware, anything. There was nothing. He went to stand in the middle of the room. "Hello?"

He heard footsteps behind him, the click of high heels. Relief spread through him.

"Beau."

He turned around as a light came on above him. Brigitte and Warner stood in the kitchen doorway, as far as they could get from him. "What're you doing here?"

"We were concerned," Brigitte said. "What the hell happened?"

Beau shook his head, checked his phone and set it on the counter. "Honestly, I don't even know."

"Warner, get him water." Brigitte crossed the kitchen toward him. "You don't look good."

"I'm fine. I mean—I'm not. I'm fucking worried. But not about myself."

Warner opened and closed cabinets.

Brigitte leaned a hip on the counter. "Start from the beginning."

"We went out to dinner. It was a special occasion, and she wanted to plan the evening. She said it was a surprise."

"What was the occasion?"

Beau opened his mouth. The occasion was private, that's what it was—him, finally getting to show her what love meant to him. Upstairs, in their bedroom, removing her trench coat. Crawling over her body as she breathed heavily on the bed, anticipating his first touch.

"That's not important," Beau said.

"I don't understand. What happened at the restaurant?"

"It wasn't there." Beau would've rather kept the details to himself, but this whole thing was getting bigger, and he was willing to sacrifice some privacy for answers. Several times over the years, he'd come to Brigitte with a business problem, and she would point out the piece of the puzzle he'd been missing. She had a surprising knack for empathy when she tried, unlike Beau. "We were at Cat Shoppe."

"You're kidding," Brigitte said, deadpan.

"I wish I were. Some way of replacing our past, I guess."

Brigitte looked at Warner. "What's taking you so long?"

"The cups moved again."

"I can get my own water." Beau remembered that Lola'd rearranged things. He wasn't even thirsty, but he went and got a glass, needing something to do with his hands. "So she had a special dance planned. She warned me not to touch her, but I thought we were playing some kind of game. Because as soon as I put my hands on her—"

She had begged him with her eyes. Tempted him with each sultry movement. He would've done anything for her in those moments, crazy for her.

"What?" Brigitte prompted. "What happened when you touched her?"

"She just…disappeared."

Chapter Twenty

Brigitte and Warner stood side by side in Beau's kitchen, quieted by the details of Beau's night. Beau drank the last of his water, set it on the counter, looked at it. Nobody spoke.

"...I moved the glasses and bowls back into their own cabinet...it's your kitchen, after all."

Lola had come into his home and disrupted his system. During the ten years Brigitte had lived there, she'd tried to do the same, but Beau'd always put up a fight. Not with Lola. He was happy she could make those little changes that made her feel at home.

Beau'd found her unprompted comments earlier about laundry and dishes adorably amusing, her nerves obviously strung tight. Her behavior had been mildly strange all day, though, up until she'd sat him down in the VIP room. She'd been collected then, as if she'd done that dance a hundred times. She *had*, but he didn't want to get that same dance. It should've made all the difference that it was him sitting in that seat.

A pit of doubt formed in his stomach. Perhaps her comments hadn't been so offhanded. Maybe they were meant to serve as a hint, something more significant than he'd thought.

He looked up from the glass. "I'm out of options. I have to call the police."

"Not yet. Just wait a minute." Brigitte played with her bottom lip. She'd been staring out the window behind him for a good two minutes, since he'd finished telling them exactly what'd happened. Brigitte went and got the cat ears from the foyer table. Beau didn't even realize he'd brought them in. "You said these were just hanging on your driver's side mirror? And her phone's disconnected?"

"Yes."

Brigitte's expression changed, her eyebrows angling inward. Beau didn't get looks of pity often. "Beau…"

"Never mind." He picked up his phone again. He had more phone calls to make, starting with the LAPD. If Brigitte was going to tell him this wasn't an accident, he didn't want to hear it.

"I think—"

"I don't care what you think." He focused on scrolling through his contact list. "You don't know the whole situation."

"Warner, give us a minute." Brigitte waited until Warner had left the room to come over and touch Beau's forearm. "Come upstairs with me before you call anyone. I want to see one thing."

Beau hovered his thumb over the call button.

"If I'm wrong, we'll call the police."

Beau returned his phone to his pocket. "What's upstairs?"

She left the kitchen, and he followed. Before reaching the second floor, she glanced back, as if to make sure he was still there. In his bedroom, she opened the closet's double doors. She ignored Beau's side and went to Lola's dresser. The top drawer was full of lacy undergarments.

"Is it all there?" Brigitte asked.

"How should I know? I don't keep track of her fucking panties." Beau went deeper into the closet as Brigitte shut the drawer and checked the one underneath it. "What are you looking for?"

She didn't answer. Beau sifted through Lola's dresses and touched the peach-colored one he'd bought her for their evening at the ballet. For once, he'd gotten her out of black—her go-to, safety color. She'd looked stunning. Good enough to eat—and he would've, had he had the chance. He slid the smooth silk through his hand. Any excuse he could think of to touch her that night, he'd used. She'd let him, up until a certain point, and then she'd politely moved his hand away and said, "Beau, you promised." He couldn't count the number of times she'd said that to him. Yes, he'd promised, but he was only a man, not a fucking saint.

Brigitte was at the bottom drawer now. She slammed it shut, squatted on the floor.

"Brigitte, I'm wasting time."

"I don't know. Maybe I'm wrong. It looks like all her stuff is here."

"Why wouldn't it be?"

She didn't look up at Beau, and that made him nervous. Normally, she delivered any news with a tremor of excitement. "I mean—the cat ears, the lipstick mark, choosing Cat Shoppe for a special occasion…it's almost like a message. A 'fuck you.'"

Beau's ears static-crackled when he swallowed. It sounded like Brigitte was suggesting Lola'd gone out of her way to hurt him, but that wasn't possible. He had no doubt Lola loved him. "You think she set me up?"

Brigitte picked at nothing on the carpet. "I think nobody gets over being hurt that bad as quickly as she did."

"She wasn't over it. We were working on it."

"Still." She looked up. "She moved in here two days later."

Beau took a step back. It didn't sound like Lola. She didn't lie or manipulate. She wasn't malicious. She would never do to him what he'd done to her.

Would she?

He wiped his temple with his sleeve. "Maybe she's still angry, and maybe she wants to hurt me. That I can wrap my head around. But not planning it ahead of time to the point you think she would've packed a bag." He shoved a finger toward the dresser. "All her shit's here."

"I don't see her personal things."

"She only came here with one bag," Beau said. "She left everything else at Johnny's."

Brigitte shook her head slowly. "I'm talking about irreplaceable stuff. Passport, license, social security card, birth certificate. She wouldn't've left those things behind."

"She didn't. I have them. I filed all that in the study when she got here."

"Is it locked up?"

"No. I wanted her to have access to…" Beau narrowed his eyes. His chest was burning, most likely from the steak. That, or his body knew something his mind refused to register.

"You hate Cat Shoppe. She knows it's a night you'd prefer to forget, and she made you relive it. That woman—you hurt her. Bad. You didn't break her heart, Beau—you put it in a goddamn blender."

"I'm not denying—"

"Have you slept with her since then?"

He paused. Were they clues, her rabid efforts to keep him at arm's length, the kisses that sometimes felt off? His face heated. Was it possible, after making him wait like a fool, that she'd never planned to sleep with him?

"Not your business," Beau said.

"Fine." Brigitte stood. "Check the study."

"I will. Only to show you you're wrong." Beau left the room, went downstairs. Lola wouldn't do this to him. Not after the progress he'd made the last few weeks. Not after he'd promised her he would do better. *Be* better. He had a lot of work to do, but it was early. What were a few rocky weeks when they had their whole lives to figure this out? Leaving him when he'd just let her closer than anyone'd ever been—it was unfathomable.

He opened the door of his study too quickly, accidentally knocking it against a wall. One drawer of the file cabinet sat ajar. He went directly to it, opening it all the way.

His heart hammered up against his chest. Lola's folder of paperwork was empty. He pulled it out, dumped it upside down. Nothing. He dropped it. The other files belonged to him, but he proceeded to check each one for something of hers, also tossing them when he found nothing. Anything important to Lola was gone.

"Gone," he said.

"That's what I thought," Brigitte said behind him.

He shoved his hands in his hair, grabbing it in two fists. There were papers everywhere. Lola was gone. She'd pulled the rug out from under him, and this was all she'd left behind—a mess at his feet. Why? To punish him for loving her?

He yanked the drawer all the way out, scanned it one last time for any stray papers, then threw it on the wood-paneled floor with a deafening *clang*. "What the fuck?"

He'd made the grave mistake of underestimating her. He'd thought the game was over. He'd waved his white flag too soon.

He was losing control. He didn't care. He wanted to lose it. He was the master—and she'd played him. She'd turned predator into prey. Without thinking, he slammed his fist into the steel cabinet. Satisfied by the throb in his hand, he did it again and again.

"Beau," Brigitte cried over the noise, "you have to calm down."

He turned on her. She had her palms over her ears. "Calm down? You want me to *calm down*?" He'd let himself *love* her. She'd pretended to *want* that from him. She'd made a fool of him *twice*, and nobody got away with that. He overturned the entire file cabinet, smashing it on the floor. "Do you have any idea what she's put me through?"

Brigitte held her hands out. "It'll be okay. I'll get Detective Bragg on the line. He'll find her—"

Beau laughed hollowly. "You think I want to *find* her?" He picked up a *Young Entrepreneurs* award from his desk and launched it against the wall, shattering it into a million little pieces. "I hope I never see that fucking bitch again."

Brigitte covered her mouth. She was trembling. "Beau. Brother. Go upstairs and rest. I'll bring you ice for your hand. None of this will seem as bad in the morning."

Rest? That was the last thing he needed. Maybe an all-night bender, or a grueling session on his treadmill. But it wasn't his body he wanted to punish.

"What's going on?" Warner asked, entering the study.

Beau went to his bar cart. "Get out. Both of you."

"Sir—"

"We aren't leaving you," Brigitte said. "You're not in the right state to be alone."

"*Don't tell me* what I am or am not. I'm not your goddamn puppet." He poured himself a generous helping of Scotch and turned his back to them, wired with adrenaline. "Do me a favor, Brigitte. Get her shit the fuck out of here. By the time I come out of this room, I want Lola completely erased from this house."

"Beau—"

"If I see anything of hers," he continued, "I will go into a rage like you've never seen." He looked over his shoulder at her. "Is that what you want?"

Warner moved in front of her, but she stopped him with a hand on his bicep. "No."

"Then *get rid of her.*"

"I will." She nodded slowly. "I'll handle it. The housekeeper will come first thing tomorrow and scrub this place until it's shining. Just promise me you'll calm down."

"Get out."

Beau returned to his alcohol once they'd gone and the door was shut. He finished his drink off in one large gulp and poured another. Lola would've needed nerves of steel to pull a stunt like this with someone like him. He'd told Brigitte he never wanted to see Lola again— that wasn't true. Not by a long shot. Just like anyone who screwed him over, Lola had to pay for this. And he wanted to be there when she did.

Chapter Twenty-One

Beau wasn't any calmer by his fourth drink. Slumped in a desk chair in his study, he'd replayed the entire evening twice already, more and more certain he'd been set up.

Lola had been quiet since they'd left the restaurant, and he could feel her eyes on him as he drove, even though his were focused out the windshield. "What's wrong?" he asked.

"What?"

Beau looked over at her. She was fidgeting with the cat ears in her lap. He still wasn't sure how he felt about this whole thing, but she seemed more excited than he'd seen her in a while. "You've been staring at me."

"Oh." She paused. "I was just thinking about how this is our last night like this."

"Like what?"

Beau drank more. She'd never answered him. Or if she had, he couldn't remember what she'd said. The alcohol was making his brain mercifully fuzzy.

He'd centered his phone on the desk, staring at it. It never rang. He'd been toying with an idea, one he hadn't been sure about, but with each drink it sounded better. He couldn't sit there anymore and do nothing. He wanted to know where Lola was, where exactly she was going to undress, shower, lay her head tonight. It was unclear to him still what he'd do with that information, but at the very least, it would give him some of his power back.

He dialed a number he hadn't used in a while. He'd already wasted enough time doing nothing.

A man answered. "I told you before—"

"I know what you told me," Beau said, "but this time it's personal. I need someone I can trust." The line was silent. "Are you there?"

Detective Bragg hacked into the phone. "I'm here. All sixty-eight years of me."

"I'll make it worth your time."

He grumbled. "My rate doubles during retirement."

"Fine."

"Triples when I'm woken up in the middle of the night."

"Don't push it, Bragg. It's only eleven."

"Middle of the night for me. I went to bed hours ago."

Beau waited through another coughing spell.

"That's what happens when you disturb an old man's sleep, Olivier. So what's this personal business? Brigitte? Your mom?"

Beau stared down into his drink. The policeman-turned-private-detective was the only person he trusted with important matters. "Why do you assume that?"

"You got nothing else personal. You don't got a wife, so she ain't cheating. No kids, so it isn't a runaway teen. There a cat in your life I don't know about? Check the trees—I hear they like to climb."

"Jeff," Beau warned.

"All right." He heaved a sigh. "Go."

Beau picked up his Scotch, stood and paced his study. His shoulders were already loosening. "You're going to find someone for me, and it has to be tonight. She won't be very far yet."

"She?"

"Yes. A woman."

"What woman?"

"Do you need to know?"

Bragg cleared his throat. "Guess not."

"One minute I was talking to her, and the next she was gone."

"When was this?"

"About an hour ago."

"As in sixty minutes? Hang on while I grab a pen. I haven't even shit out what I had for dinner yet. An hour's nothing, kid."

Beau massaged the bridge of his nose. It *was* nothing. An hour was a long time in his and Lola's story, though. He'd only actually known her two or so months. Lola was beginning to seem like a wild dream, a hallucination brought on by a night fever. Something untouchable.

"Got my pen," Bragg said. "Shoot."

"Her only family in the area is her mom. She works at The Lucky Egg diner in East Hollywood."

"What about the girl? Where's she work?"

"She left her job at Hey Joe on Sunset Boulevard a few weeks ago."

"Think the folks there'll know anything?"

Beau spun his drink on his desk. It wasn't impossible that Johnny knew something. Veronica too. Maybe Lola *had* mentioned something to her, and they were all in on it. They weren't friends to him. Fuck, Lola might've stopped there to say goodbye. Maybe she was there now. Beau could be there in twenty minutes, and with money as leverage, he could have Johnny talking in twenty-five.

Johnny responded to threats, but Beau didn't. He wasn't going to play Lola's game and track her down himself. He was an important man. He hired people like Bragg for that.

"They might know something," Beau decided. "Her ex-boyfriend works there. Start with him."

"Going to tell me how to do my job? You want to do this yourself, be my guest."

"I've got better things to do," Beau said. "That's why I'm paying you."

Bragg muttered something into the phone. "All right. Tonight—what's the last place you saw her?"

Beau's mind went to the strip club, Lola's hips swaying within his reach. She was in her element there, sexy as hell. Just like the night her sweet, red mouth had lovingly eaten his cock the first time. "Cat Shoppe. It's a strip joint, also on Sunset Boulevard. You know the place?"

"What do you think?"

"I'm not allowed in there, so don't mention my name until you know what you're dealing with." Beau rubbed the skin above his eyebrows. "On second thought, maybe you should start there."

"Sounds like you got ideas on how to do this, which is fine since the clock's ticking. You go talk to the boyfriend, and I'll hit the strip club."

"No. Like I said, this isn't worth my time."

"And like *I* said, don't tell me how to do my fucking job. So what else you got?"

"That's everything. She's got black hair, blue eyes." And she'd leave you with an impression that stayed no matter how many times you tried blinking it away. Like glimpsing the sun. Beau grit his teeth against the thoughts he wanted to shut out. "Don't worry, Bragg. You can't miss her."

"I'll start with the titty bar after I get something going on her license plate number and credit cards."

Beau took another long gulp of his drink, welcoming the burn of alcohol down his throat. He set the tumbler on his desk. "She doesn't have a car."

"Don't tell me that."

"No license plate. She could be on the goddamn city bus for all I know."

"The bus? She's a slippery one, eh?"

"Apparently."

"How about a name? She got one of those?"

"Right. It's Lola. Lola Winters."

"Lola…Winters," he repeated slowly as if writing it down. "Middle name?"

A middle name? At times, he'd thought he'd known Lola inside out. He'd anticipated her every move, directed her, surprised her. Once in a while, though, he was reminded how little he knew. Like the girl she'd been before Johnny, how many kids she wanted or even if she was a dog or cat person. He'd never thought to ask her middle name.

"I don't know."

"How about a cell number?"

Beau rubbed the back of his neck. "She doesn't have one of those either."

"Let me get this straight. You want me to find some chick who's got no job, no car, no cell. And she disappeared into thin air?"

"I called you because you're the best."

"Yeah, well—the best is going to cost you, Olivier."

"Bill me." Beau hit 'End' and put his phone away. It was only a matter of time now before he had her back. The question was what he'd do with her.

BOOKS IN THE

Explicitly Yours Series

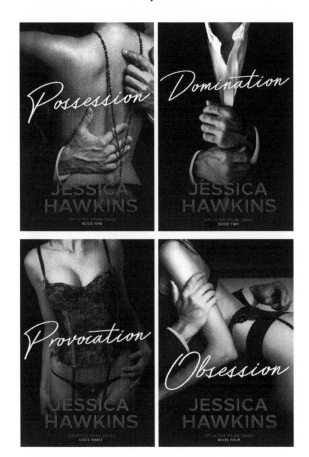

TITLES BY
JESSICA HAWKINS
LEARN MORE AT JESSICAHAWKINS.NET/BOOKS

SLIP OF THE TONGUE
THE FIRST TASTE
YOURS TO BARE

THE CITYSCAPE SERIES
COME UNDONE
COME ALIVE
COME TOGETHER

EXPLICITLY YOURS SERIES
POSSESSION
DOMINATION
PROVOCATION
OBSESSION

STRICTLY OFF LIMITS

ABOUT THE AUTHOR

JESSICA HAWKINS grew up between the purple mountains and under the endless sun of Palm Springs, California. She studied international business at Arizona State University and has also lived in Costa Rica and New York City. To her, the most intriguing fiction is forbidden, and that's what you'll find in her stories. Currently, she resides wherever her head lands, which is often the unexpected (but warm) keyboard of her trusty MacBook.

CONNECT WITH JESSICA

Stay updated & join the
JESSICA HAWKINS Mailing List
www.JESSICAHAWKINS.net/mailing-list

www.amazon.com/author/jessicahawkins
www.facebook.com/jessicahawkinsauthor
twitter: @jess_hawk